Guardian's Nemesis

Anna Gabriel Book 3

Georgia Wagner

Text Copyright © 2024 Georgia Wagner

Publisher: Greenfield Press Ltd

The right of Georgia Wagner to be identified as author of the Work has been asserted in accordance with the Copyright, Designs and Patents Act 1988

All rights reserved.

The book is copyright material and must not be copied, reproduced, transferred, distributed, leased, licensed or publicly performed or used in any way except as specifically permitted in writing by the publishers, as allowed under the terms and conditions under which it was purchased or as strictly permitted by applicable copyright law. Any unauthorised distribution or use of this text may be a direct infringement of the author's and publisher's rights and those responsible may be liable in law accordingly.

'Guardian's Nemesis' is a work of fiction. Names, characters, businesses, organisations, places, events, and incidents either are the product of the author's imagination or are used fictitiously. Any resemblance to actual persons, living or dead, and events or locations is entirely coincidental.

testament to the pride of the townspeople. Anna noted a small cafe with lace curtains fluttering in the light breeze and an old barbershop with a striped pole spinning lazily.

Beth turned to her, a smile tugging at her lips. "It's cute."

Anna grunted in response, scanning their surroundings as they made their way to the motel she had booked online.

Clearwater was a strategic choice—an attempt to slip beneath the radar, to exchange one set of dangers for the obscurity of a small town. The FBI agents swarming Mammoth Lakes had been too close for comfort.

Sniper school had taught her patience. Demolitions school had imparted precision. SEAL school had instilled resilience. But none of them had prepared her for the kind of war she waged now—a subtle battle to protect her baby sister.

Beth deserved her protection after everything she'd been through... after Anna's failure to protect her sister's family.

Anna's left hand tightened around the wheel, the same strong grip that could fire a weapon with lethal accuracy. She drew in a slow breath as the RV labored up a slight incline, the engine's low groan a testament to the miles they had covered.

Five years out of the game, and yet these last weeks, it felt like she'd never left. The shadows of past operations clung to her like a second skin, impossible to peel away. Here, in Clearwater, she hoped for a reprieve—for hers and Beth's sake.

The turn signal clicked rhythmically as Anna eased the RV into the gravel lot of the Pine Haven Motel. Dust from the road settled slowly.

"Guess this is home for now," Beth murmured, her gaze drifting across the peeling paint of the motel sign.

"Home," Anna echoed. She killed the engine and the silence that followed was heavy.

"Could be worse," Beth said, offering a smile, strained but genuine.

"Could be," Anna agreed, allowing herself the flicker of a half-smile in return. "Remember, comfort isn't the priority. Safety is. And safety means blending in." She fixed Beth with a serious stare, adding weight to the words. "We're just another pair of travelers passing through Clearwater."

"Right," Beth said, swallowing and blinking as she nervously tried to match the gravity of her sister's words.

Clearwater was an insular town, but Anna hoped that two sisters passing through wouldn't raise many eyebrows.

She'd often found people underestimated her due to her gender. It was a simple bias that a couple of men drifting into town would more likely draw the scrutiny of the local police—more likely be assumed *dangerous*. But two adult women? Sisters on a trip? No one would expect the sort of deadly force Anna could bring to bear, or that Beth, thanks to her training with Casper, was now capable of.

And that was just the way she liked it.

They exited the RV, the doors shutting with solid thunks behind them. The air was cool, carrying the scent of pine and earth. Anna's boots crunched on the gravel as they approached the motel office.

"Good evening, ladies," greeted the clerk, a young man with a too-bright smile and hair that fell over one eye. He leaned forward, elbows on the counter, interest piqued. "What brings you to Clearwater?"

Anna, as she was accustomed to, didn't reply right away, but rather took in the appearance of the clerk: he had greasy blond hair, an earring glinting in one ear, and a tattoo peeking out from under his sleeve. His eyes lingered a moment too long on Beth, who returned his smile with practiced politeness.

"Just passing through," Anna finally answered, her voice measured. She held out a pad of folded bills, and the clerk raised an eyebrow. "We're the ones who phoned ahead about a 'cash only' price," Anna added quietly.

Anna had never believed in plastic, and she knew all too well how people could abuse the types of systems that kept people's names, addresses, and details all in tight, neat columns. It sometimes made navigating the world difficult, and she'd used fake identities for temporary cards from time to time to rent cars or set up hotels, but whenever she could, Anna still preferred the anonymity of cash.

The clerk let out a breathy sound of recognition and tapped his nose. "Right, right," he said. "Room for two then?"

"Two beds," Beth clarified, leaning into the counter space. "We have a reservation."

"Of course." He processed the transaction with practiced ease, handing over the keycard with a lingering touch and a smirk that didn't quite reach his eyes. "Room 219. Second floor, end of the hall."

"Thanks," Beth smiled, accepting the key from Anna's outstretched hand.

"Say," the clerk said quickly, "Clearwater ain't really on the way to anywhere. You sure you got the right place?"

"It's that rustic tourism," Beth said, still cheerful and friendly, playing the part effortlessly.

"We're here to see the sights," Anna added, her tone making it clear she had no interest in continuing this conversation.

But the clerk didn't seem to take the hint.

"Really? Not much to see around here." The clerk's eyes lingered on Beth, a twinkle of mischief in his gaze.

"Sometimes, less is more," Anna interjected, her voice even, her eyes scanning the small lobby. A mounted deer head. A rack of outdated travel brochures. A coffee machine with an 'Out of Order' sign taped crookedly to its front.

"Ah, a philosopher," he quipped, returning his attention to the computer screen. "Well, enjoy your stay. And if you need any... local recommendations," the clerk added with a wink, "just ask for Mike."

"Will do, Mike," Beth nodded.

"Say!" Mike said quickly, reaching out as if to catch Beth's arm, but then thinking better of it. "Don't mind me asking, you ever been in town before? I know I'd recognize you."

Beth just smiled, shaking her head. "No, haven't been."

"Well, then," Mike said, rounding the side of his clerk counter and settling so he was now standing closer, his back leaning against the raised lip of the counter. "Why don't I show you the best parts of this place."

Mike had an easy smile, and a stray finger reached up to brush aside some of his greasy hair. Beth just smiled politely, giving a small noncommittal nod. She had this effect on the opposite sex—Anna had often noticed it growing up. Blonde hair, pretty features, friendly disposition, Beth drew the eye, as the saying went.

But right now, the attention was a threat.

She cleared her throat, shot a frown towards Mike, and guided Beth away, out the office door again.

Once outside, Anna exhaled sharply, the tension in her shoulders easing fractionally. She grunted, nodding towards the second level of the motel doors facing the road. They climbed the stairs side by side, the metal steps groaning under their weight.

"Probably should keep to ourselves," Anna said quietly.

"I wasn't trying to chat him up."

"I know. Wasn't saying you were. Just... still, good to keep to ourselves."

Beth nodded absentmindedly.

The second-floor corridor greeted them with a stale scent of cleaning chemicals and old smoke. Fluorescent lights hummed overhead, casting stark shadows against dingy walls. They passed numbered doors, all closed, until muted thuds reached Anna's ears from behind one of them. Her eyes narrowed.

"Did you hear that?" Beth's voice came low, her steps faltering.

"Keep walking," Anna said without breaking stride.

A man's shout, muffled but intense, sliced through the thin walls. Beth's frown creased deeper, worry etching into the lines of her face.

"Anna, that doesn't sound good."

"None of our business." Anna's words cut the air, decisive, cold.

Beth hesitated, hand hovering as if to knock, but then she caught Anna's stern look. A silent communication—they needed no more trouble, no more complications. They had enough of those already.

They moved on, toward their own door at the end of the hallway. The shouting was a fading echo now, just another part of the motel's ambiance. Anna slid the keycard through the reader, a green light flickered, a click followed.

Safety first. Never get involved—a lesson she kept learning the hard way. And this time, she refused to fail it. Not when her sister's safety was on the line. There could be no involvement, not in Maine. That was the rule, the only way to survive. Anna Gabriel knew that better than anyone.

The click of the door unlocking was drowned out by a sudden surge in volume from the neighboring room. A deep voice boomed, followed by something heavy slamming against a wall. Anna's hand froze on the handle, her body tensing.

"Anna?" Beth's whisper barely reached over the growing scene next door.

Anna felt her instincts warring against each other. On one hand, it sounded as if something violent was happening in the room next door. On the other, she needed to keep Beth safe. They'd driven across the country to escape the eye of surveillance. Jefferson and Greeves, the FBI agents who had Anna in their crosshairs, had been asking around Mammoth Lakes. If Anna and Beth appeared on the radar once more, on the other side of the continent, it would entirely defeat the purpose of the relentless three-day drive.

And yet...

The voice was growing angrier still.

"Stay here," Anna said sharply, pointing at her baby sister.

"Anna!" Beth protested.

"Stay!" Anna snapped. She pushed open the motel room door, assaulted by the scent of mint air freshener.

At the age of twenty-five, her sister was only five years younger, and yet Anna felt as if they were both children again, and it was up to her to keep an eye out for Beth. Beth had always been the kinder, more naive of the two. She didn't have to peer under rocks to see what wriggly and poisoned things came out, because Anna was willing to do it for her. And Beth had it in her head that she wanted to be like Anna. She was practicing—and had been taking combat lessons from Casper back in Mammoth Lakes.

But a month of shooting and sparring does not a killer make.

As Anna listened at the door, Beth abruptly gave a huff and marched forward, slipping past her sister. In the same moment, Anna snagged her younger sister by the elbow.

"Anna, let me go!" Beth insisted.

To Anna's shock, Beth pulled her arm from her sister's grasp, approached the door, and knocked timidly. "Excuse me?" Beth called out, polite as ever. "Is everything okay in there?"

The sounds from within suddenly ceased.

Anna's heart pounded in her chest as she watched Beth knock on the door. A moment of pure silence followed, making Anna hold her breath. She wanted to grab Beth, pull her away, keep her safe. But it was too late now. The damage was done. The door creaked open slowly, revealing a man standing there, his face etched with lines of anger and frustration. His eyes flickered between Anna and Beth, assessing them silently.

The man in question didn't at all look like what Anna had imagined. He didn't resemble some drunk in a rundown motel. If anything, he looked handsome. Yes, handsome was the word, but only in a manufactured sort of way, like a car salesman. Slicked-back brown hair, tailored suit, and a jawline sharp enough to cut glass. None of his natural features were particularly noteworthy, and it was as if his face had been designed to be as inoffensive as possible—a face for TV.

The only extraordinary feature that didn't come out of a box was his eyes, piercing blue irises that locked onto Beth with an intensity that made Anna uneasy.

"What do you want?" His voice was calm, but there was an undercurrent of steel in it.

Beth took a step back, her cheerful facade faltering for the first time since they'd arrived in Clearwater. Behind her, Anna straightened up, her military training kicking in as she assessed the situation and stepped beside her sister.

"We heard shouting... just making sure everything's alright," Anna replied evenly, her eyes meeting his unwavering gaze.

The man's lips curled into a smirk that didn't reach his eyes. "No need to worry, ladies. Just a little misunderstanding. Nothing you need to be concerned about."

Anna's instincts told her otherwise. The tension in the air was palpable, and she could sense Beth's unease growing beside her.

"Maybe we should go," Beth whispered to Anna, her voice barely audible.

Anna's green eyes glanced past the man. She brushed the single streak of prematurely white bangs from her eyes, shifting the rest of her dark hair behind an ear. She studied the room in that brief moment, noting egress points and potential hiding spots. But it was clean. No sign of a fight, no one else in the room. A laptop was open on the man's bed, and it displayed the frame of a video feed.

He'd been shouting at someone on that conference call.

"Our mistake," Anna said simply.

"Yeah, it was," he snapped.

Beth grimaced as if she'd been slapped. She'd always been the more sensitive of the two.

Anna just shrugged, reaching out to grab the door handle and close it for the man. His blue gaze glanced at her bone frog and trident tattoo on her extended arm, but if he understood the significance of the SEAL team sigils, he gave no outward sign of it.

Turning back to their own room, the door shut behind them and Anna felt a wave of relief wash over her. She placed a hand on Beth's shoulder, giving her a small reassuring squeeze. The air inside the motel room felt heavy, charged with the tension from the encounter next door.

Beth sank onto the edge of the bed, her hands trembling slightly. "What was that about, Anna?" she asked, her voice barely above a whisper.

Anna considered her words carefully before responding. "Honestly, he just looked like a Wall Street type having a bad day, Beth. We don't need to get involved in his business."

Her sister nodded slowly, but Anna could see the worry lingering in her eyes. Beth was always quick to empathize with others, sometimes to her own detriment. But Anna couldn't blame her. It was one of the things she admired most about Beth—the ability to see the good in people even when they didn't show it.

As they settled into the room, Anna's mind raced with thoughts of what they were doing in Clearwater.

"Just... relax," Anna said simply. "We have to stay out of trouble, and what you did back there, that's asking for it. Got it?"

"Y-yeah."

Anna walked over to the window, gazing out at the dimly lit street below. The faint glow of streetlights illuminated the dusty road, casting long shadows across the pavement. It was a quiet evening in Clearwater, but Anna knew better than to trust silence.

Turning back to Beth, she saw her sister curled up on the bed, her eyes fixed on some distant point. "Hey," Anna said softly, sitting down beside her. "We're safe here, Beth. No one knows we're here."

"Casper said he could find Tom. The kids..." Beth looked up, eyes hopeful. "Do you know when we'll hear back?"

Anna hid her frown. She wished her former SEAL teammate would stop leading her sister on regarding the search for her lost family. Ever since Anna had asked for his help, Casper had shown a vivacity she hadn't seen from him in years. He'd lost all his retirement pudge, toned up his already impressive muscles, and taken to helping Beth like he was back in the Navy breaking

15

in new recruits... back when all of them had felt indestructible, like there was no one they couldn't save.

Anna pictured the fiery ball, the helicopter toppling from the sky. The explosion.

Tom and the kids were gone... Anna was almost sure of it. No one had seen the Albino or any of his crew in weeks. He'd gone to ground. Despite the hints and slim possibilities that Beth's family *might* have survived, eventually, Anna knew she'd have to tell her sister. To confront her with the hard truth...

But now wasn't that time.

"He's got contacts I don't," Anna said simply. "Give him time. It might be a while."

"They're out there," Beth insisted, frowning at her sister. "I know they're alive."

Anna didn't reply.

"I know you don't believe it," Beth said in a small voice. She couldn't hold her sister's gaze. "But I know it."

Anna just flashed a small sad smile.

Beth turned her gaze to Anna, her eyes filled with a mix of fear and gratitude. She nodded slowly, her blonde hair falling gently around her face. Anna could see the turmoil within her sister, the weight of their past traumas pressing down on her fragile shoulders. But in that moment, as the two sisters sat together in the dimly lit motel room, there was a sense of fleeting peace. And Anna refused to shatter it.

"I trust you, Anna," Beth whispered, her voice barely audible in the quiet room.

Anna felt a pang in her chest at her sister's words. As much as she tried to shield Beth from the darkness of their shared history, she knew that some shadows were impossible to erase. But here, in this small town of Clearwater, Anna hoped they could find a moment of respite, a chance to breathe without the suffocating grip of their past tightening around them.

"We'll figure this out, Beth. Together," Anna reassured her, placing a comforting hand on her sister's trembling shoulder.

Beth offered a small smile, the ghost of her usual cheerfulness flickering in her eyes. "I know we will," she replied softly.

As they sat in silence, the distant sound of crickets chirping outside drifted through the window, mingling with the gentle hum of the air conditioning unit.

With a deep breath, Anna leaned back against the headboard of the bed, feeling the weight of exhaustion settle.

Only as she closed her eyes, trying to relax, did something strike her as odd.

The man in the room next door's voice had sounded... different than the yelling, shouting voice they'd heard.

Had someone else been in that room?

If so, they would've had to hide under the bed. Anna had seen through the single-room unit, and spotted the open bathroom door, the mirror reflecting the shower.

No one else had been in that room.

Unless they'd been hiding under the bed...

She snorted. But who the hell would hide under a motel room bed?

She shook her head, refusing to allow the thoughts to linger.

They were safe.

For now.

Chapter 2

Beth's eyes snapped open as she started in fear.

A sound had caught her attention in the small, cramped motel room. Or had it been a dream? It had felt real enough, a sort of ambiguous scuff and thud.

She blinked, her vision clearing as she attempted to glance around, searching for... what was the source of that noise?

She frowned, shaking her head, sitting up where she lay under the window by the radiator. Her back ached, and she'd moved in the night, her head shifting off the pillow. The motel room was suffused with a murky predawn light, and the stillness of the air seemed to fracture with a noise foreign to the humdrum of nocturnal sounds. It was abrupt, a discordant scratch in the quiet that set her heart drumming against her ribs.

She lay motionless, listening, her breath a shallow whisper between clenched teeth. The threadbare carpet beneath her hands was gritty, reeking of stale cigarettes and spilled liquor. The bed beside her stood desolate, its sheets a tangled mess, the pillow dented by an absent head.

Anna was still sleeping by the door.

Beth glanced over at her older sister, frowning slightly.

Her older sister looked the very picture of comfort as if the hard, crusty carpet of the motel floor was a luxury bed. But Anna had always been able to sleep in uncomfortable locations.

Sighing, Beth stared at her sister's slumbering features... She'd often envied her sister. Anna was... tough. There was no other word for it. No... perhaps there was. Other words did come to mind. Words like, competent, confident, and unflappable.

She'd spent the last few weeks training. She could have said 'to get my family back', 'to be stronger', but really all of it boiled down to a simpler idea: 'to be more like Anna'. There was no other way to put it.

If she'd even been a tenth as competent as her sister, then her family might not—

She cut off the train of thought.

Scowling and shaking her head, Beth chose a brief spurt of irritation at her distracted thoughts over the throbbing ache of grief threatening to rise in her chest.

Through the cracked window, the cool breath of the outside world whispered in, carrying with it the scent of pine and damp earth. Indicative of the motel's upkeep, the glass was webbed with thin fractures, the largest of which stretched from the lower left corner upwards, splintering the view into disjointed shards of the parking lot beyond. Moonlight filtered through the fissures, casting jagged shadows across the floor.

A hushed rustle came from the curtains as they fluttered with the breeze, their edges frayed and tinged with the yellow of nicotine. And with it came a dull, distant thud.

She frowned—the sound had come from outside.

She edged closer to the window, the cool air kissing her face. There—movement between the trees. A man.

The neighbor from next door.

She recognized his slick hair, and he was still wearing that expensive suit. He was scowling, though, his face twisting into something like a demonic mask.

Gone was the cocksure, suave air of the man who'd answered the door earlier. This man's face was like melted wax, twisted and turned in horrible ways. And as he passed under the window, moving through the trees, she heard him speaking. He tried to keep his voice to a whisper, but it was a hissing hushed tone, intercut with the scuff of his shoes as he paced and the dull thud of his hand intermittently patting the motel wall.

His voice cut through the stillness, sharp, urgent, fancy business suit out of place against the backdrop of untamed woods. A hand clutched at his phone, his words indistinct and swept up in the night air.

"Damn it!" His tone spiked, a single phrase reaching Beth. A problem. A big one, by the sound of it.

Her breath fogged up the windowpane as she leaned closer, her forehead almost touching the cold glass. The man turned, phone still pressed to his ear, his profile etched with lines of anger or perhaps fear. Hard to tell. And for a brief moment as the man paused, he turned and—before she could duck out of sight—he was staring right at her.

She froze. His blue eyes pierced her, holding her in place.

The man scowled again, and then turned, moving off into the woods with the determined strides of a man late to catch his train.

Beth watched him leave, unable to look away. Fear spiked in her, blood pounding in her ears. But why?

Because she'd been caught looking?

She felt a flicker of anger. Why was she always so scared? Her hands bunched at her sides.

"Anna," she whispered but swallowed back the rest of the words. Her sister, a warrior in slumber, deserved these scant moments of peace. No. She would not wake her. Not yet.

Little Beth couldn't always go running to big sister.

Her fingers curled into a fist. Resolve hardened like ice within her chest. Anna had fought battles across continents, faced lethal foes in shadowed battlegrounds dozens if not hundreds of times, and here she was scared because a well-dressed man had sneered at her.

The man had vanished into the woods.

He'd frightened her, then disappeared.

A scowl reappeared on Beth's face. How dare he. How dare he try and scare her?

She snarled, her lips twisting. No... no, she refused to be frightened. He had no right.

Now... now she was done with fear.

Done with men like the smarmy man in his stupid suit.

She laced up her boots with the same swift and silent pull as an assassin with a garrot. Beth's fingers gripped the cold metal latch, her movements deliberate and silent. She pushed against the window, the frame groaning in protest, a whisper in the otherwise hushed room. The gap widened just enough for her to squeeze through. Her eyes locked onto the pattern of shadow and moonlight playing across the deteriorated outer wall of the motel.

One breath. Steady. In. Out.

She hoisted herself up, finding purchase on the worn ledge beneath the window. Beneath that, an old air conditioning unit protruded like a rusted offering. It held her weight. Just. A loose brick served as the next step, jutting out from the facade. Her muscles tensed, those same muscles developed by carrying two children at her hip around the house, around the store, up the stairs. A stay-at-home mother... She'd never been ashamed of the role. It had made her strong. She'd seen Casper's shock at how well she took to the training, she'd surprised herself even, and now that strength was leaner, more focused.

She descended.

GUARDIAN'S NEMESIS

The ground met her with a muffled thud of her boots. Eyes adjusting, she crouched low, scanning the darkness. The faint glow of a phone screen bobbed between the trees—her beacon, her target. Her jaw set. No words now, just action.

Beth slid into the night, keeping close to the shadows that clung to the base of the motel. The rough bark of an oak tree bit into her palms as she steadied herself against it, peering around the trunk. The light from the phone was moving away, slow but purposeful.

She followed, though she couldn't have said why she followed. Maybe just to prove her new skills, to show herself that Anna and Casper's lessons—on how to carry herself, how to move discreetly and purposefully, how to stay calm in spite of fear—that all those lessons had taken root, that she could do it in the real world too.

Her footsteps a silent dance over the gravel and pine needles scattered along the path. Distance measured in heartbeats. Closer. Closer. Her focus narrowed to the man's back, to the pale light he cradled against his ear.

Each step she took was a muted affair, a testament to the hours spent honing her ability to move unseen, unheard. Beth's breathing remained even, controlled, despite the adrenaline that thrummed through her veins.

Clearwater's namesake lake loomed ahead, a silent expanse shrouded in the night. Beth's steps slowed—a cautious approach. Water lapped at the shore. She crouched behind an old, gnarled tree, its branches bare and reaching out like the fingers of a skeletal hand.

What was making the man with the phone so angry?

There he was, his silhouette cut against the faint moonlight reflecting off the water. He paced a short stretch of the lakeshore, phone pressed to his ear, his voice a hiss of urgent whispers carried away by the wind. Beth studied him, his expensive suit now seeming out of place amidst the wild backdrop.

Time stretched thin as she watched, her eyes never wavering. The man stopped pacing. His head cocked to one side, listening. Silence fell heavy around them, broken only by his one-sided conversation. A hushed argument. A demand. His free hand slashed through the air, punctuating invisible points.

Beth's muscles tensed, ready to react. Her mind raced, trying to piece together fragmented clues from the gestures of his shadow.

He was saying something... she crept closer, hiding behind the trees, somehow certain that she couldn't let him see her. Not now. It wouldn't end well if he spotted her.

The man was hissing now, "If you ever want to see him alive again... Yes... Yes, I already told you. No, dammit. That's not how this works. Do you want him back? Hmm? *Do* you?"

Beth stared, then frowned. What had she stumbled upon?

The man in the suit was shaking with rage. "I'll gut him while you watch! Do you hear me? I'll gut him. You better—"

And then it happened.

The man's body stiffened. The phone slipped from his grasp, crashing onto the pebbles at the water's edge. He swayed—a tall tree in a sudden gale, roots giving way. He collapsed. No cry. No sound of struggle. Just the soft thud of a form hitting the ground, the finality of it sending ripples across the stillness of the lake.

Shock jolted through Beth. She blinked, expecting motion, a sign of feigned collapse. But there was nothing. Only the man, crumpled and still, and the quiet hum of the night reclaiming its territory.

The phone had gone quiet.

Instinct kicked in. Beth's protective nature took over as she dashed to the man's side, her heart hammering against her ribs. The night air was cool, but her palms were slick with sweat as she reached for his neck, searching for the pulse that would indicate life. Her fingers pressed into his skin, but no rhythmic thump greeted her touch.

"Come on," she muttered, a whisper lost to the night. No answer from the man. No flutter under his jaw. Nothing. A heart attack? Aneurysm? People don't just 'drop dead'.

Suddenly remembering herself, Beth spotted his phone lying a foot from the man's stiff fingers. She stared at it while she took one more steadying breath then picked it up.

"P-please," a voice was crying. "Just let me speak to him. I just want to know my little boy is alive. Please..."

Beth hesitated, frozen in place. The dead man had been threatening to kill this woman's child. But now what? What should she do? What *could* she do?

She was panicking now, holding the phone tightly. She didn't speak at first.

"H-hello?" The voice on the other end sounded so forlorn. So desperate. A voice that mirrored the ache in Beth's own chest. A voice that cut like a knife.

"Hello?" Beth whispered.

"Sammie? Sammie, is that you?" the voice said suddenly, horrified.

"N-no... Who's Sammie?"

A pause. Then click.

The line went dead.

Beth stared at the phone in her hand. Sammie... who the hell was Sammie?

She turned her attention back to the man on the ground.

Beth's eyes narrowed, scanning for injuries—a bullet hole, a knife wound, anything. But the moonlight revealed no mar in his suit, no dark stain to indicate violence. Just a body, perfectly dressed, inexplicably dead.

For one wild moment, she thought he was faking.

But no... no, she'd felt with her own hands. The man didn't have a pulse.

Her mind raced. Questions without answers. Why? How? But logic told her time was not a friend. The water lapped at his legs, threatening to claim him in a quiet embrace. She couldn't leave him there. Evidence. Clues. They might wash away with the current.

She grasped his shoulders, the fabric of his suit slipping slightly in her grip. With a grunt, she heaved, pulling him away from the water's edge. Every muscle strained as she dragged the dead weight across the pebbles and sand, away from the lake that seemed eager to swallow him whole.

Once clear, Beth paused, her chest heaving. She looked down at the motionless figure, the face unknown yet hauntingly familiar in its stillness. Death had a look. A look she knew too well.

"Damn it," she breathed out, steeling herself.

What the hell was she supposed to do now? Her sister's words about 'asking for trouble' rushed back to her mind, and Beth winced, feeling for a moment like a shamefaced child who'd just made a mess in the kitchen. But that was silly. A man was dead, and that voice on the phone desperately asking for Sammie—something terrible was happening here.

Anna. She needed Anna. They had to move fast.

Beth's breath tore through the silence, her feet pounding the gravel as she sprinted back to the motel. The night air was sharp, biting at her lungs, but panic fueled her strides. She had to get Anna.

The dim glow of the vacancy sign flickered as she approached, casting long, creeping shadows across the parking lot.

She darted in. The creepy clerk, Mike, sat behind the counter, reading a dirty magazine. He glanced up as she entered. "Well, hello there," he said, grinning wolfishly.

"No time, sorry," she said.

She sprinted to the stairs.

Her heart hammered in her chest, each beat a drum of urgency. She reached the second floor, then reached their door, her hand slamming against the wood, loud, insistent.

"Anna," she called out, her voice a hoarse whisper and a shout all at once. A moment passed. Two. Too long. "Anna!"

The lock clicked, and the door swung open. Anna stood there, alert, her eyes searching Beth's face for the crisis written there.

Beth was briefly taken aback by just how calm Anna looked. It didn't seem as if she'd even been sleeping. She looked alert, composed...

How did she do it?

"Man in the woods," Beth gasped, words coming in short bursts. "Dead. No wounds."

Anna's posture shifted, every line of her body coiled spring tight. She was awake, aware, the soldier within seconds.

No further questions. Simple trust in her sister's urgency, then an attempt at a solution.

"Show me," Anna said.

Chapter 3

Anna stared at the body.

The Gabriel sisters stood under the watchful moon, shoulder to shoulder, inhaling the scent of the lakewater, and the fragrance of petrichor brought on by morning dew.

"He just fell here," Beth said, as if eager to break the silence. "I didn't touch him."

"What about after?" Anna shot her sister a sidelong glance.

"Ummm. Yeah... yeah, after... I was trying to make sure he was okay."

"I see." Anna left it at that.

"Y-you're not mad, are you?"

Anna didn't reply right away. What would the benefit have been? She was furious, of course. How could she not be? Beth should've just stayed put. Should've left well enough alone.

And now they had a dead man on the doorstep of their motel. A man they'd spoken with the night before, and a man who Beth's DNA and fingerprints would likely be all over.

"No," she said quietly. "I'm not angry."

"I know when you're lying," Beth said in a small voice.

Anna sighed, shaking her head. "I'm not mad, but you might be."

"W-why?"

"Because of what we're going to do. Here, grab his legs." Anna was already reaching for the man's arms.

Beth stared at her sister, stunned. "What are you doing?"

Anna just grunted, already picking up the man by the wrists. "Your DNA and prints will be all over him. He's *dead,* and the two of us are going to be interviewed by every cop in the area if our names show up anywhere near this. The FBI will be on us in seconds."

"S-so... what are we going to do?"

"Simple. Get rid of the body."

"Anna!"

"Beth?"

"We can't do that."

"Sure we can. Grab the legs."

Beth just gaped at her sister under the moonlight, appearing very much like a landed trout. "Anna! We need to—"

"Call the police?" Anna asked, looking over the body at her sister. "Really?"

A huff of air. "No... but... Why can't we tip them off anonymously?"

"Your prints and DNA, sis. And we were in communication with him last night. Thanks for that, by the way. If anyone overheard our little conversation, they might even tell the cops we 'argued' before his death."

"Won't this just make us look worse?"

"If they catch us," Anna said simply. "They won't."

"How can you be sure?"

"Because I'm really good at hiding things that are never found." Anna added, under her breath, "Some might say I've had a lot of practice. Now, grab his legs."

"I think... I think he hurt someone."

"What?" Anna looked up, exasperated now. She tried to keep her emotions in check. Civilians needed calm or they panicked.

"He was talking on the phone with someone. Making threats... Like he was going to hurt someone. I... I talked to someone on the phone."

Anna's eyes whipped over. "Wait, what?"

"Not long. It was more like... I just picked up the phone."

"What did you say?"

"I don't remember."

"What did they say?"

"Asked if I was Sammie... I think... I think this man hurt someone named Sammie."

Anna sighed, rubbing the bridge of her nose.

"The woman on the phone... she sounded terrified. What if Sammie is her child?" Beth said, her voice trembling.

Anna lowered her hand. This, of course, was why she'd felt a sudden weariness. Beth had a heart of gold, and so of course it would come out when they needed to keep a low profile.

The thought of someone else's child in danger was simply too much for Beth, but Anna was here to protect her sister.

She exhaled slowly, staring out.

The lake was still, a mirror to the waning moon. Anna's boots sank into the soft earth at the edge of the water. And then, instead of speaking, she returned her attention to the task.

"One thing at a time," she said.

Hands firm on the dead man's wrists, she dragged the weight with a steady, practiced gait. Reluctantly, her sister grasped the man's legs, and followed Anna's lead. Beth panted, her grip faltering on the ankles. The man's body arched unnaturally between them.

"Keep it up," Anna said, her voice low and even.

Beth grimaced, her thin arms trembling under the strain. She nodded, biting down on her lip as she steadied herself. Each step betrayed her struggle; Anna's did not. The difference in strength was not just physical. It ran deeper. The idea of hiding a body didn't faze Anna. It was just another task in the mission. Prioritize. Execute.

But for Beth...

This was uncharted territory.

They reached the necessary spot, hidden by drooping branches and the veil of night. With a final heave, they deposited the corpse onto a bed of detritus.

Now, the body was hidden in the woods. No one would stumble upon it.

Phase two came next.

"Stay here," Anna commanded, already turning away.

"Where are you going?"

"Need something to finish the job. Stay here."

Anna turned away, hurrying back in the direction she'd come from.

Anna approached the motel parking lot, her movements a ghostly glide across the pavement. Her gaze flickered, taking in the positions of security cameras with an assassin's precision. She retrieved a hose from around the side of the motel, near a faucet. A jerrycan leaned against the basement door, amidst other, older, rusted containers.

In the parking lot, she found an old truck, its gas cap unlocked. Quick and silent, Anna fed the hose into the filler pipe. Mouth to the opening, she sucked the hose briefly, gasoline fumes biting at her throat before liquid flowed freely into the jerrycan. No spills, no scent left behind.

She scanned the area once more, every sense alert for the hint of movement, the whisper of fabric, the scent of another human. Nothing stirred but the distant hum of a highway.

Satisfied, Anna replaced the cap, wiped down the hose with a cloth, and retreated. The can heavy in her hand, she moved back through the darkness, a predator evading capture. But as she passed the front of the motel... she hesitated.

Her eyes slipped towards the opening, and she bit her lower lip. Her gaze slipped up the trellis to the second floor.

The security cameras prevented any access through the front door... but she could reach the second-floor window easily enough.

She hesitated only briefly... Who had the man in the suit been shouting at last night? Who else had been shouting?

She'd heard another voice in his bedroom. She was nearly sure of it.

Anna's shadow merged with the night as she edged along the motel wall. The place was a relic, peeling paint and neon flickers promising vacancies that nobody wanted to claim. Her eyes traced the path of the security cameras, black domes like unblinking eyes that she deftly avoided with practiced ease.

She reached a small wall in the back of the motel, and above, she spotted the open window to their room. Next to it, a second window, this one sealed shut. And it would lead to the dead man's room.

A glance left and right. No one was watching. Setting the jerry can at the base of the wall, she reached out, snagging the brick wall and pulling herself up.

The rough texture of the brick gave Anna's tough fingers good purchase and she ascended the wall with uncanny grace. Every movement was calculated, every breath controlled. She hoisted herself up onto the windowsill, her muscles taut with tension.

She pressed her hands against the glass. The window wasn't latched. It slid up as she pushed, her hands feeling the slick cold surface.

Peering into the darkened room, she scanned the shadowed space cautiously. The dim moonlight filtering through the curtains revealed a disheveled interior, devoid of any occupants. The air held a stale tang.

As she swung one leg over the sill to gain entry, a creak from within made her freeze. Instinctively, Anna withdrew, pressing her back against the wall outside. Her heart thudded in her chest as she strained to catch any sound from inside the room.

Silence and the errant night sounds of Maine filled the air around her once more. With a steely resolve, Anna resumed her ingress into the chamber, but slower, more cautiously. Her boots touched down on the worn carpet without a sound as she surveyed the surroundings with sharp eyes.

Room 217.

The room swallowed her whole. Stale air. She gave a few intent sniffs, picking a faint, acrid odor. Bleach.

The bed. Unmade. Sheets twisted. Amidst the chaos of fabric, photographs scattered like fallen leaves in autumn. She approached, crouched beside the bed. Her fingers, calloused and steady, picked up a photo.

A young boy. Tears streaking dirt on his cheeks. Eyes wide with an emotion that clawed at Anna's insides. Fear. Desperation. She sifted through more photos, each snapshot a moment of the boy looking lost and forlorn, wearing a puffy, blue jacket and red shoes. Expensive shoes, by the look of them.

"Who are you?" The question escaped her lips, a whisper to the absent child.

She pocketed one photo, the weight of it heavy against her thigh.

Anna pivoted on her heel, her gaze sweeping the room. Walls barren, save for a peeling wallpaper that suggested neglect. A single lamp cast shadows that danced with her every movement. She took measured steps, her trained eyes scanning for anything out of place, any sign of the boy with the tear-stained face.

The closet door stood ajar. She tugged it open with a cautious hand; empty hangers clinked together like skeletal fingers. No clothes, no suitcase. Nothing to indicate someone was staying here.

She slid the top drawer of the dresser open. Empty. The next, the same. Her movements quickened, a growing impatience threading through her methodical search. Third drawer, nothing but a Gideon's Bible, its pages untouched, the spine uncreased.

A motel room scrubbed clean of personal touches. No toiletries, no stray socks. No half-filled cups of coffee or crumpled receipts. It felt staged, sanitized.

"Where are you?" she muttered, her voice barely disturbing the heavy silence that enveloped the room.

The bed. She dropped to her knees, left hand reaching under the mattress. The space there yielded nothing but dust bunnies and the stale scent of old sweat.

But then, there... She frowned. In the shadow, pressed against the leg of the bed near the window.

Anna lay flat, the carpet rough against her cheek. Her arm extended into the darkness. Fingertips brushed paper. Then metal. Items crammed in the shadow beneath the headboard. Her heart skipped. She pulled out the items one by one, laying them out before her.

Cash. Bundles bound with rubber bands, edges crisp. Too much for a casual traveler. Next, a Maine driver's license. The picture was of the man they had just left in the woods. The plastic printed name referred to the dead man as Jim Monroe.

"Hi, Jim," Anna muttered, turning the flimsy card in her fingers.

But why wouldn't someone like Jim keep their license in their wallet? The easy answer was that this wasn't Jim's real license. Forgery wasn't Anna's specialty, but she felt the uneasy suspicion settling that the crisp, clean ID in her hands wouldn't check out. Meaning Jim Monroe may not even be their mystery man's real name.

With a sigh and a flick, Anna dropped the card back into the small pile of cash. She turned her attention to the final item in the cache, a heavy, well-oiled Glock 17. She knew it well—standard issue for someone trained to kill.

Anna's pulse quickened. Cash. Fake ID. Gun. Tools of her former trade. They whispered of something more sinister than a random criminal act.

"Who were you running from?" Her question floated, unanswered.

Questions churned in her head. Why was this man here? Who was the crying boy? What had they stumbled into?

Hands steady, Anna reassembled the findings, tucking the cash and ID back into their hiding place. For the gun, she took the extra precaution of wiping it down with the bed sheets, careful about leaving any trace of a print before depositing it back in the cache.

Something was off in all of this... Something that ate at her.

Where was the man's laptop?

She'd seen it on his bed when they'd first confronted him at his door. So where was it now? Anna glanced around the room once more, but she was running out of time. Morning would come soon, and Beth would be worrying.

Anna returned by the window, moving swiftly now. She shouldered her jerry can of pilfered gasoline and hastened away from the quiet motel, avoiding the pools of light cast by the few functioning lampposts, and cutting through the chill air in a brisk jog.

When she arrived back at their hidden place in the woods, she found Beth waiting, faithfully, her silhouette a smudge against the backdrop of the lake. Anna approached, her sister's eyes finding her own in the dim glow of the moon.

"What's that?" Beth's voice was low, tense.

"Gas," Anna said simply.

Beth blinked. Then her eyes widened in horror. "You're not serious."

"Fire is the perfect way to destroy DNA and fingerprints."

"I didn't kill him, Anna!"

"I know. But no one else will. Now, back away," Anna instructed, her tone leaving no room for protest.

Beth frowned back in petulant defiance, her face momentarily returning to a shape familiar from their childhood, but after a few seconds she complied, retreating several steps.

Anna poured the gasoline over the man's body, making sure to cover every inch. She reached for her lighter, her thumb brushing against the flint wheel. She hesitated for a moment, looking back at Beth's face. It was pale and drawn, eyes wide with fear and disbelief.

Anna took a deep breath, trying to ignore the knot of unease that was growing in her chest. She knew she was doing the right thing, the practical thing, the safe thing for her and her sister. But it didn't make it any easier.

By all evidence, the man at her feet wasn't a very good one. Besides, her mission was to protect Beth.

She struck the lighter, the flame flickering to life. She held it close to the gasoline-soaked body, watching as the liquid caught fire and began to spread. A hiss escaped her teeth as she took a step back, glancing at Beth once more.

Flames erupted, greedily consuming the gasoline-soaked clothing. Heat blasted their faces, the firelight painting their features in stark relief. They watched the body burn, the evidence turning to ash, the DNA evaporating into the night.

"Who was he?" Beth whispered, the question hanging between them, unanswered.

"Doesn't matter now." Anna's response was flat, her eyes never leaving the blaze.

The fire crackled, popped, a pyre for secrets. Shadows danced on their faces, a tango of light and dark.

Anna turned now. "Let's go," she said quietly.

"Where to?"

"RV. We're leaving."

"Won't... that look suspicious?"

"Depends when they find the asshole."

Beth stared at the body on the ground, looking as if she wanted to be sick.

Anna was moving, though, and Beth fell into step.

"Sammie... we can't leave him out there."

"We don't even know who Sammie is," Anna shot back.

She tried not to picture the face on the photograph she had in her pocket. She'd intended to send it to Casper—her old SEAL buddy—and have him ask around.

"We can't just leave," Beth said hurriedly as she hastened after her sister over the pine-needle strewn ground.

"Enough." Anna's voice was terse, clipped. "It's done. We walk away."

"Anna," Beth's plea cut through the crackling of cinders behind them. "Sammie could be in danger."

"Or dead," Anna said, but regret laced her words instantly.

"Then we owe it to whoever his mother is," Beth shot back, her jaw set.

"Owe? We owe nothing. I'm here to keep you safe, Beth."

"The way you kept my family safe?" Beth shot back, her voice sharp.

The words stung. They'd been designed to, and they'd succeeded.

Almost instantly, Beth apologized. "Sorry."

Anna didn't reply right away. The words hurt, but in her experience, there was no point in lashing out over such words. Usually, the pain meant they carried a grain of truth, and she felt a flutter of frustration and discomfort at the thought.

Beth stepped closer, her shadow merging with Anna's. "I'm sorry. Really, I am. I shouldn't have said that. I know you're only trying to help. Just... he's a kid, Anna."

Silence stretched between them, taut as a tripwire. Memories flickered behind Anna's eyes, unwanted guests. She swallowed them down.

"Damn it, Beth, it's not our fight."

Beth just stared at the side of her sister's face.

"It's not!" Anna insisted, louder.

But her hand strayed to the photograph in her pocket. The boy with the expensive red shoes stared out from the memory of the image, haunting her with his gaze.

She released a slow, pent-up breath.

"You can still get in a world of trouble when you're trying to do the right thing. And there's nothing we can do."

"We can check," Beth said.

"Check what?"

"His phone." Beth's hand slipped into her pocket, revealing the man's sleek phone. She handed it over to Anna without a word.

Anna hesitated, then sighed in defeat as she took the phone. She flicked the screen on, seeing it was locked. Her brow furrowed as she tried a few common passcodes, but none worked. Without missing a beat, she pocketed the phone.

"Come on," Anna said, turning away from the burning remains behind them. "Act casual. Pack quickly and don't touch anything you don't have to. It's better if they forget we even stayed here before your friend's disappearance is noticed."

Beth fell into step beside her, eyes fixed on the ground as they walked back toward the motel. The night was still and heavy around them, and Anna felt her sister's anxious energy rolling off her with every step up to their room.

"Well?" Beth whispered, as they shouldered their meager luggage and cut back for the parking lot.

"Well what?"

"The phone," Anna's sister prompted.

"Phone's locked."

"Can we unlock it?"

"Maybe."

"What about Waldo? He's good with phones."

Anna bit her lower lip to hold back her initial retort. The eccentric conman had a way of fraying her nerves, contradicting her at every turn, while somehow also delivering magic whenever he put his mind to a task. It was like working with a mischievous genie from a kid's story, and Anna could feel her blood pressure spike at the mere mention of the frazzle-haired Waldo Strange the Third.

Spotting her RV in the parking lot, they walked swiftly towards it, trying not to think of all the ways the path they were taking could end in disaster.

Beth wanted to find Sammie, a child she only imagined from the panicked voice on a mysterious phone call, a boy who may not even match the picture of the tear-stained child in Anna's pocket.

Anna just wanted to leave, to keep herself and her sister safe.

They drove in tense silence, pulling away as the sun slowly rose ahead of them, Anna's stomach clenched as she tried to ignore the picture in her pocket. If she got what she wanted, this could all be a bad memory by sunset. What was one more nightmare?

She looked to Beth, her sister's far-away stare already settling into a scarred-hardness that Anna was all too familiar with, and an uneasy tension settled in Anna's chest. One of the things that set them apart had always been Beth's softness. It was why she had had a family, why her heart was bleeding right now for a child she'd never even seen. Anna wanted to protect her. But what kind of protection was it if she let her sister become as hard... as calloused as she was?

Anna let out a soft hiss, snatching up her phone with one hand as the other tightened on the wheel, swiping through her contacts with her thumb and moving the receiver to her ear as she inwardly winced.

"Waldo... I have a favor to ask."

Chapter 4

Sammie crouched in the pitch-black room, the rough strands of the rope biting into his palm. Each clench sent stabs of pain up his arms, the raw skin of his wrists screaming with each movement. He pressed his back against the cold stone wall, the damp seeping through his thin shirt.

He winced, glancing down at the red marks around his wrists. He looked across the room at the small chair. Rope fibers could be seen scattered around the ground.

They hadn't tied it very tight, and his father... He nearly bit back a sob at the thought of his dad. But his father had taught him knots from a young age... As an Eagle Scout, Sammie knew his way around ropes.

And traps.

Now, the rope that had once bound his wrists was lying across the ground in front of the old, wooden door.

He waited, listening, trying not to let panic overtake his thoughts.

Footsteps. Approaching. Thuds against the wooden floor outside grew louder. His heart thumped against his ribcage, a drumbeat in the silence. Fear clawed at his insides, whispering for him to find a shadow, a corner, any refuge from the danger that neared. But he pressed his small body more firmly against the wall. Still. Silent.

The steps halted just beyond the door. Sammie's breath hitched. The urge to flee, to dissolve into the darkness, surged. Yet he pictured his father's face, stern and unyielding in the face of threat. Be brave. Sammie tightened his grip on the rope. His resolve hardened like the ice on a winter lake.

He waited. His chest rose and fell. The footsteps resumed. Closer. Closer still. Sammie braved a glance at the sliver of light beneath the door. A shadow cut through it. He swallowed the lump in his throat.

"Stay put," he whispered to himself, the words barely a puff of air. "Be brave." The footsteps stopped again, right outside the door. Sammie exhaled, slow and controlled. His small fingers curled tighter around the rope, knuckles white.

The door creaked, a slow groan of old hinges. A voice cut through the stillness, deep and falsely soothing. "It's all gonna be over soon, kid. Just quit crying, alright?"

Sammie's jaw clenched. Silent. Motionless. The rope lay in his hands, deceptively casual. His heart hammered against his chest with the force of a caged animal fighting for freedom. He counted the seconds, each one an eternity stretching into the next.

Sammie had forgotten to move the chair... It was well within the line of sight of the doorway.

Oh no.

He felt his heart skip.

"What the hell..." the man in the door muttered.

He'd seen the chair.

The figure stepped over the threshold, a massive, ogre-like outline. Towering. Imposing. A dark shape against the dim light filtering from outside the room so large that the floorboards complained under his weight.

Sammie waited, every muscle coiled. Time slowed. The figure took a step forward, staring in bewilderment at the empty chair.

Now.

With a surge of energy born of fear and desperation, Sammie yanked hard on the rope. The figure's foot caught. There was a grunt, then an explosive crash that hit the silent room like a thunderclap as the man hit the ground.

"Damn kid!" The shout was tinged with anger and surprise, echoing against the walls.

But Sammie didn't wait to hear more.

His small feet hit the ground running. He leapt through the air, and the man beneath him groaned, arms flailing to regain balance. But Sammie was already past him. He pictured how many times in gym he'd failed the high jump test—he wondered what Coach Lintz would say if he could see how much air he cleared now.

His bare feet slapped the wooden floor, each step a sharp crack in the otherwise silent basement. Adrenaline surged through his veins, obliterating thought, enhancing instinct.

"Get back here!" The man's voice boomed from behind, thick with rage and the pain of his fall.

The hallway loomed dark and foreboding, stretching out like a tunnel to uncertainty. Sammie's breath came in quick bursts, his chest tight with exertion. Shadows clung to the walls, but he pushed forward, eyes darting side to side, desperate for a sign, any indication of a way out.

"Stop, or I'll shoot!" The threat sliced through the air, a cruel promise.

No time to consider it. No time to freeze. Sammie charged on, the idea of stopping as foreign to him now as the concept of surrender. The hallway seemed to narrow, the darkness pressing in, but there—there at the end—a sliver of hope.

Stairs.

He could hear the man picking himself up, the shuffling of heavy feet, the rustle of clothing. Sammie's small form flickered through streaks of moonlight that found their way into the hall, casting an eerie glow on his path to potential salvation.

He took the stairs two at a time, ignoring the creaks that begged for caution. Each step propelled him closer to freedom, each rise and fall a beat in the rhythm of escape.

Up. Up into the darkness above, where freedom waited, just out of grasp.

The wood groaned under his weight, protesting each urgent footfall. Every fiber in his body screamed for release, for the open air that promised life beyond these walls. His mind held a single thought: reach the top.

He refused to think of how he'd ended up here...

He refused to remember what they'd done to his father...

He felt a sob forming on his lips, but pushed it aside with a final surge, one hand grasping the cold metal rail.

He hit the final step. The cellar door stood before him, a barrier between captivity and the world outside. Muscles aching, lungs burning, Sammie seized the cold metal handle. It gave way with an agonizing creak.

Air. Fresh, morning air flooded his senses. The scent of pine and earth mingled with the crispness of impending dawn. Above him, the moon hung low—a silent sentinel in a sea of stars. Freedom lay mere inches away, shrouded in the shadows of towering trees.

Sammie didn't hesitate for a heartbeat. He pushed through, emerging from the bowels of his prison into the embrace of the forest night.

Leaves crunched under Sammie's feet. He darted between the trunks, his breaths coming in short bursts. The night was a maze of darkness and whispers, but he didn't flinch. Each sharp stab from the uneven ground below fueled his need to move faster, to put more space between him and what he left behind.

GUARDIAN'S NEMESIS

Thick branches snagged at his clothes, clawing like the hands he had escaped. He twisted away, kept running. His bare soles were raw, every stone and stick a new bite of pain. But there was no time for pain.

A twinge of fear prickled as he noticed his naked feet. The vulnerability of his flesh against nature's unforgiving floor.

"Keep going," he whispered to himself, the only encouragement in a world reduced to shadows and fear.

Sammie's feet pounded the uneven forest floor, a relentless rhythm against the night. Pinecones cracked under his weight, needles pricking his soles like thousands of tiny daggers. Pain shot up his legs with every footfall, yet he couldn't stop. Wouldn't stop. He had to create distance — every inch mattered.

Behind him, a shout shattered the silence. Deep. Menacing. The large man was still there, still chasing. Fear gripped his chest, squeezing tighter with each echo that bounced off the trees. It spurred him on, forced his legs to pump harder, despite exhaustion weaving its way into his muscles.

"Stop, boy!" The words rolled through the darkness, a promise of danger if he didn't obey.

But the pursuing footfalls were another promise.

Danger if he stopped.

Sammie knew he was quickly running out of options, and there was nothing left to do but run at a dead sprint into the dark, night-time forest.

Chapter 5

The glare of the sun off the RV's windshield did little to mask Anna's furrowed brow as she glared at the screen before her. Waldo Strange the Third's shit-eating grin filled the rectangular box on her tablet propped against the steering wheel.

Beth sat at Anna's side, gaping at the image on the screen, trying to hold back a laugh. Anna simply contented herself with scowling at the man.

Once, he'd promised her the location of someone who might be able to locate the Albino, the man who'd kidnapped Beth and her family.

But then he'd asked for a fee.

Fifty thousand dollars. Anna didn't have that type of money, and she wasn't about to ask Beth—her sister had already cashed out the insurance on her home and was dealing with too much already.

Things had gone cold between them. Anna had resisted the urge to beat the information out of Waldo.

She knew he was a liar, and besides... She had her own theories about what had happened to Beth's family. Beth still held out hope they'd somehow survived, but Anna... Anna held out very little hope for such an outcome, and she didn't see the point in leading Beth on.

Better for a clean break, a new start.

And so they found themselves in Clearwater.

And now Waldo came with a white streak in his hair, grinning at her. "You consider my offer from before?" he said, wiggling his eyebrows. "Fifty thousand for the location—"

"Cut the crap, Waldo. Explain the hair," Anna snapped, her back pressed rigid against her RV's seat, her head having popped off the headrest as Waldo came into view on the video call. She didn't want him to drag Beth into this, and so she used a sharp tone to redirect the conversation.

Next to her, Beth held the phone they'd taken from the dead man. Evidence. If ever they were caught, holding that phone would get them both thrown away.

GUARDIAN'S NEMESIS

But right now, Anna was distracted by the lanky conman on the video feed.

Waldo leaned back in his chair, a smirk playing on his lips. His eyes always held mischief, and his jaw and cheekbones had always been pronounced on account of his astoundingly low body-fat percentage.

But his tousled hair, which he never so much as combed, looked different now.

For one, he had a single streak of white dyed in his bangs.

A streak of white that looked suspiciously similar to Anna's natural streak.

"It's just age, darling. Happens to the best of us."

"Since when did age hit you overnight?" Her tone was ice, eyes narrowed slits as she watched him through the digital divide.

"The muse never sleeps, Anna."

Beth was desperately trying to hold back a sound of mirth as Waldo flipped his hair from his eyes, running a hand through the white streak.

Anna exhaled slowly, counting to five in her mind, and attempting to calm her temper.

She grabbed the phone from the passenger seat, its black surface smeared with fingerprints. Holding it up to the camera, she thrust it towards Waldo's virtual face, her left hand steady despite the mounting irritation. "Can you open this remotely?"

"Always straight to business." A chuckle escaped Waldo's throat.

"Can you do it or not?" The words came out clipped, each syllable a bullet.

"Your charm never ceases to amaze me," he quipped. "Would it hurt to try 'please'? 'Thank you'?"

"I don't know, but I know a thing or two that definitely hurts."

"Oh. Sounds like a threat."

"Stop flirting and answer my question."

He snorted. "You flatter yourself. But alright, alright." His fingers danced across his own unseen keyboard, the clatter a faint sound in the background. "I'm emailing you an app. Download it on your phone and then hold your phone up to the locked one."

Anna felt her stomach clench. "Waldo, if you—"

"It's nothing weird! Scout's honor. I'm just piggybacking your phone's signal so I can tinker with the target."

"While giving you access to my phone," Anna interjected flatly.

"Where's the trust?" Waldo winked, then rolled his eyes. "Look. You want this done fast? This is how we do it. Otherwise, you can drive out here and hand me the phone in person, send it parcel post, or—"

Anna pinched her nose with a groan. "Ok. I get it. Fine. Send me the app."

"Already sent."

The attachment with Waldo's custom program looked as sketchy as it felt, and Anna's phone warned her twice before she could disable enough safety features to install it. When she held her phone up to the dead professional's locked screen though, both lit up and Waldo's app gave a pleased chirp.

"Alrightio, looks like I'm hooked up," Waldo said pleasantly, twirling his freshly-dyed white streak in one finger as he stuck out his tongue in focus. "Just keep your phone charged and turned on, and don't let it get too far away from the locked phone or I'll lose the signal."

Anna sighed. "Oh, is that all?"

Waldo sat up indignantly, his hand flapping his chest in mock affront. "Hey, I'm performing an honest-to-god digital miracle here. Can I at least get that 'thank you'?"

"How long will it take?" Beth asked, leaning forward anxiously as Anna's lips drew into a hard line.

"Patience, my lady. A day. Maybe two. It depends on how hard it's going to be to get into his device. Now—" His eyebrows wiggled as his gaze strayed in Beth's direction. "Anything else I can help you lovely ladies with?"

Beth didn't know the entirety of Waldo's involvement in her family's disappearance. Waldo hadn't intentionally been malicious. He'd tried to run a con, and people far worse than him hadn't taken kindly to his meddling.

But the thought of Waldo trying to schmooze her younger sister only irritated her further.

Thoughts of Beth always brought thoughts of her missing family. Her husband, Tom, and her two children: five-year-old Tony and three-year-old Sarah.

Beth was leaning forward eagerly, staring at the screen, and Anna didn't have the heart to put up any more of a fight.

She knew why this was such a big deal to Beth, anyhow.

If she could find this Sammie, and reunite the child with whoever had lost him, then maybe she'd find a happy ending to her own story.

The thought of it caused a pang in Anna's heart.

She found her hand slipping to her thigh and reaching into her pocket to withdraw the photograph she'd stolen from the dead man's bedroom.

Anna's fingers fumbled with the creased photograph, and she held it up to the camera, a tremor creeping into her steady sniper-trained hands.

"Recognize him?" Her voice was an arrow, straight and sharp.

Waldo's eyes narrowed, his usual smirk replaced by a furrowed brow as he leaned toward the screen. "What's this?"

"Just tell me. You spend a lot of time doing nothing on your couch. See anything about a kid like this on the news?"

"Hurtful," he replied. "Closer; can't see it properly."

The photo moved closer, paper edges almost brushing against the webcam. A young face stared back through the digital window.

Anna had been expecting another wiseass remark, so when Waldo reacted, she was taken aback. "Shit," Waldo breathed. The charm wiped off his face like fog on a windshield.

Anna's heart hitched. "What? Who is it?"

Waldo's words came slowly. "You're in Maine, right?"

Anna frowned. She didn't confirm it. She hadn't told anyone where they were going.

"How do you know that?" Beth said.

Anna grit her teeth, shooting her sister a withering glance, but Waldo was already replying. "Because... shit, when Maine makes national news, everyone notices."

"Maine made the news?"

"Yeah... hang on." A clack of keyboards. He was nodding. "Mhmm... see, I watch a news channel with the latest conspiracies. It's a blast."

"Waldo, get to it."

"Yeah, well, they had a picture of that kid," Waldo said, his finger pixelated as it hovered on the screen, evidently pointing. "That's the dead mayor's son. Sam, something. He's missing."

"Sammie?" Beth said, perking up.

"No, no, that's not it," Waldo said.

Beth was on her phone now. "It says right here," She said, her voice coming in a gasp. "It's Sammie Henderson. His dad, Mayor Greg Henderson, was murdered. Sammie's missing."

A chill shot through Anna's spine. Missing. Dead mayor. The connection spun webs in her mind, sticky and confining. Her throat tightened. "Missing how?"

"Vanished," Waldo said, his tone now devoid of any traces of jest. "His dad's not even in the ground yet—you know, murder investigation and all. But the kid?" Waldo gave a shrug and a sad shake of his head.

Shock rooted Anna to the spot, a statue with a racing heart.

"Any leads?" she managed to ask, though her voice seemed to belong to someone else.

"None. It's like he evaporated. And now you're holding his picture." Waldo's gaze pierced through the screen, searching for answers in her reaction.

Anna glanced up, scanning the lot around her RV like the cracked canvas of some inscrutable painting. But no one approached their RV, for now.

"Tell me about the mayor," Anna demanded, her eyes narrowing at the image of Waldo, his streak of white hair now a serious slash across his otherwise youthful appearance.

"Dead," Waldo replied, voice flat like the thud of a judge's gavel. "No signs to say why or how."

"Dead." Anna repeated the word. It tasted bitter. "And the boy?"

"Missing, like I said," Waldo insisted.

Anna felt Beth's gaze on her back, heavy and expectant.

"Missing how?" she pushed.

"No one knows. Are you hearing me or am I muting myself? I could've sworn I already told you everything I know."

"No need to be a wiseass."

"Not so much an issue of need as nature," he quipped back. But it seemed more habitual than anything as his face had lost its earlier amusement, now etched with lines of concern.

Anna's breath caught in her chest. A dead man with no cause of death. A boy gone without a trace. The weight of it settled on her shoulders, cold and unyielding.

"Are you sure they don't know the cause of the mayor's death?"

"Nada," said Waldo. "Least that's what the online stuff keeps saying. A real what-done-it. That's a thing, right?"

Anna was shooting Beth a look, though, willing her sister not to say anything about the man from last night. Also dead. Also without any evident cause.

What was happening?

Anna's fingers grazed the cold, metallic surface of the phone as she turned it over in her hand, the cold plastic and circuitry that held the potential to unlock a mystery. Her gaze lifted to Waldo's expectant face on the screen.

"Fine," she muttered, the word slicing through the static silence of the RV. "Just get this phone open, okay?"

"I'll do my best. No promises. Just remember—"

"Keep it charged, on, and close to my phone. Got it." Anna took a steadying breath, giving Waldo a nod through the video call. "Send me what you find," she added, already rising from her seat.

The morning sun was now fully over the horizon, the day officially begun.

And things were only getting stranger.

Who had killed the mayor? Who had taken his son, Sammie?

And who was the dead man from last night?

Anna felt the pressure of his phone against her leg, and she let out a slow, huffing breath of air.

"We need to get going," Anna said.

"We're not leaving town," Beth replied sharply.

Anna turned to her sister. "We're not going to be of any help," Anna said.

"Why not?"

"No... as in, we won't be. We don't have the resources the cops do. Feds will be on this one too. A dead mayor?"

"And a missing child," Beth murmured.

"We should go. We really should."

But Beth just stared at the dash.

"Beth... Please. There are a couple of other cities with low surveillance profiles. One's only a few hours from here. We can make it before noon."

"I'm staying, Anna."

"Beth... Seriously. My job is to keep you safe."

"Then stay with me. I don't want to fight." Her sister took a shallow breath, shaking her head and reaching for the door handle. "But I'm not leaving. If you're so scared of the FBI though, maybe you *should.*"

Beth began to rise, the door popping with the motion, but Anna growled under her breath, lunging out and jerking the door closed.

Scowling at her sister, Beth snapped, "What? Are you going to tie me up?"

For a moment, Anna was tempted to do just this.

Anna's jaw clenched, her frustration simmering beneath a facade of cold resolve. She released the grip on the door, her sharp gaze locked on Beth. "I'm not leaving you here," she stated firmly. "Especially with everything that's happening. It's not safe for you."

Beth's eyes flickered with a mixture of defiance and concern. "I'll be fine, Anna."

"I can't let you go running around on your own, Beth. Not with all this going on." Anna's voice was firm, laced with worry and frustration. She knew Beth was mama-bear levels of determined, but this time, the stakes felt too high for an argument.

"Let me?" Beth said, her tone sharp.

"You know what I mean."

"I'm afraid I do." Beth sighed, her shoulders slumping slightly. "I'm not a child, Anna. But there is one out there who needs help."

"Beth, there are a lot of children in the world who need help. Right now, Casper is trying to find your family. And I'm trying to keep you safe until that happens. We need to lay low. It's as simple as that."

But Beth didn't back down. She kept her hand extended towards the door.

Rubbing her temples in exasperation, Anna studied her sister's face. The lines of determination were etched deep within Beth's expression.

"I'm staying. You can leave."

Beth wasn't backing down. So, Anna released a slow sigh.

"Fine, let's just stick together for now," Anna said, her tone softening. "We'll figure out our next move together."

"I already told you what our next move is."

"Fine... fine, but if Waldo can't unlock that phone... We give it to the cops anonymously and we leave."

"And if he can?"

Anna hesitated.

"What if he can, Anna?" Beth insisted.

She bit her lip. She knew when the odds were stacked against her, and so Anna released a slow breath. She shrugged. "In that case... I'll do what I can to help."

Beth looked pleased, but Anna cut this off with a comment of her own, "And if he can't... will you agree to hand this off to the locals? We get out of here?"

Beth hesitated for a moment before nodding in reluctant agreement.

Anna released the door and settled back into the driver's seat of the RV. The weight of the situation pressed down on her; the intertwining mysteries of a dead mayor, a missing child, and the strange man from the motel room demanded her attention.

As the engine roared to life and the RV rolled out of the gas station parking lot, Anna's mind flashed back to the cache of money, Jim Monroe's fake ID and Glock, the faint tinge of bleach on the air. Everything about the man they'd burned in the woods made her uneasy, like pieces of a puzzle far darker than her younger sister could understand. And a truth that might destroy the little hope Beth was clinging to.

Because Sammie hadn't been in that motel room.

Chapter 6

Anna was inwardly kicking herself. She should've known better than to make that deal with Beth.

She'd counted on Waldo's lackadaisical nature and unreliable self. But she supposed she had to hand it to the conman.

The one time she didn't want him to come through, he had.

And now, Anna found herself staring at the phone in her hand and holding it up to compare the address on the device, to the meat-packing plant beyond the chain-link fence.

"Shit," she muttered under her breath.

"Is this it?" Beth asked excitedly, leaning forward from the seat next to Anna, and staring at the screen.

She tapped a finger against the number of the address. "Two-seventy-eight," she said. Her finger then pointed to the fading letters on the commercial building's concrete placard. "Two-seventy-eight. This is it. This is where they're keeping Sammie."

Anna nodded once.

The dead man's phone hadn't been the cornucopia of information Anna had hoped for. It had a single app installed, displaying a lump sum transfer of over twenty-thousand dollars. And it had an address, sent via anonymous text.

The transfer hadn't been traceable according to Waldo, but the address?

Local.

And now the two sisters sat in the RV, peering out the windshield towards the meat-packing facility. A faint stench of blood and decay lingered in the air, carried on a cold breeze that swept through the area. Anna's mind raced as she took in the grim surroundings, her instincts on high alert.

"We can't just barge in there," Anna said, her voice blunt.

"You said you'd help."

"I know. I will. Just..." Anna trailed off, lowering her voice to a controlled, neutral tone before continuing. "Whoever that man was back at the motel, he was a hired gun of some sort. A hitman, probably."

"You think... think he killed the mayor?"

Anna glanced sharply out the window, wincing. "I don't know."

"It's strange, though, isn't it? Both of them died without any apparent cause."

"Could be a rare toxin. Could be something that attacks the heart."

"Yeah... yeah, probably." Beth frowned, glancing towards the meat-packing facility once more.

She had a compassionate heart, but Anna could tell Beth's mind was fixated on the living, not the dead.

"We don't know Sammie is in there," Anna said.

"Yeah, but the text... Why else would this address be in a hitman's phone?"

Anna hesitated. She briefly considered explaining the idea of dead drops and code locations, but instead, she swallowed her words.

"Fine," Anna murmured. "But you're staying here."

"Okay."

Anna blinked, stunned. "What? As easy as that?"

Beth nodded once. "I've been training with Casper, and I'm not as helpless as I was... But I know I'm not you." Her mouth quirked, tugging into a shallow grimace as if the words were bitter to taste. "I've accepted that you don't want to be here, and I don't want to get in the way."

Anna hesitated, frowning. "Are you just telling me what you think I want to hear?"

Beth blinked, then smiled sweetly as she reached out and touched Anna's arm. "Thank you, Anna. Thanks."

Anna just nodded. She felt a wave of relief. She'd expected that conversation to be much more difficult, but Beth was reasonable. Anna had agreed to help find Sammie, but they were going to do it as safely as possible.

Which meant Beth needed to stay out of the line of fire.

"Here," Anna said, reaching for the glove compartment where she kept her spare sidearm.

Anna handed the pistol to Beth. Her tone was firm as she spoke, "If anything happens, stay in the RV. Lock yourself in and don't come out until I get back. Understood?"

Beth took the gun hesitantly, her fingers brushing against the cool metal. She nodded, her eyes reflecting a mix of determination and fear. "Understood," she whispered.

Anna gave her a reassuring smile before opening the driver's side door and stepping out into the cold morning air. The sky was brighter now, the moon barely visible through the thick clouds that loomed overhead. As she made her way towards the meat-packing plant, Anna pulled her own sidearm from its holster, rapidly checking the slide and safety with a quick series of metal clicks.

The chain-link fence that surrounded the facility rattled in the wind, creating an eerie soundtrack to Anna's footsteps. She moved quietly, her senses on high alert for any signs of danger. The building itself was old and rundown, with broken windows and peeling paint giving it a sinister appearance.

Anna's shadow melded with the darkness as she edged along the perimeter of the meat-packing plant. Her hand, calloused and steady, hovered near the pistol holstered at her side. The other hand traced the cold metal fence, fingertips reading the ridges and bumps like braille. She paused, listened. A distant hum of machinery played counterpoint to her slow, measured breathing.

Eyes narrowed, she scanned for the telltale glint of camera lenses, and then in a blur of movement, she climbed over the fence and dropped down the other side, landing nimbly.

She moved towards the main building in a swift, controlled dash.

The service door loomed ahead. She tried it. Locked.

A frown creased her face and she glanced towards a large window set in the wall near the door.

She didn't hesitate. Moral choices had to be made on the fly at times, but most of the time, decisions were made before the mission. Hesitation could get one killed.

Her elbow slammed into the glass with precision, shattering it with a clattering sound. Anna paused for a heartbeat, her green eyes scanning the interior of the room beyond.

No reaction. No alarm.

Darkness enveloped the space, broken only by faint rays of early morning sunlight filtering through the grime-coated windows.

Stepping through the broken glass, Anna landed in a crouch, her combat boots absorbing the impact noiselessly. The room smelled of rust and old machinery, sending a shiver down her spine. She straightened up slowly, her senses on high alert as she assessed her surroundings.

Metal hooks lined the walls, dangling ominously like twisted fingers in the dim light. A row of industrial-size freezers hummed in the background, casting eerie shadows across the floor. Anna's jaw clenched as she moved silently through the room, each step calculated and deliberate.

Corridors stretched out before her, dimly lit by flickering fluorescent lights that cast elongated shadows on the concrete floors. The air was thick with the metallic tang of blood, a scent that no amount of industrial cleaner could erase. It clung to the walls, to the floor, to the very air she breathed.

Silence enveloped her save for the occasional drip of water from an exposed pipe. Anna's boots made no sound on the damp floor; they were soft-soled and well-worn.

Above her, rows of meat hooks swung gently from steel tracks bolted to the ceiling. They glinted dully in the sparse light, remnants of flesh clinging to some, a morbid testament to the plant's purpose. Each hook seemed to eye her as she passed, winking in the first rays of sunlight.

She moved through the corridors, with slow, patient steps.

Her breaths came even and controlled, despite the chill that clawed at her spine. The plant was a tomb at this hour, a repository for carcasses both animal and, if her suspicions were correct, possibly human.

What sort of bastard would hide a child in a place like this?

What if they were wrong? What if the hitman wasn't the one who had Sammie?

No... no, given what she'd heard on the phone, the picture she'd found... Anna bet he was deeply involved.

Briefly, she frowned, picturing the scene in the motel room. Someone else's voice had been yelling. Now, though, she wondered if it had been someone else on the computer screen. What if the hitman had been in contact with his employer?

Did that make sense?

None of it really did. Not yet.

Then, she heard the sound of footsteps. Voices.

Anna paused, her back pressing against a cold metal wall. She peered around the corner, eyes narrowing. Two guards, weapons at the ready, patrolled the hallway ahead. Their boots thudded with a steady rhythm against the concrete floor, a discordant heartbeat in the silent expanse of the plant. The presence of armed men wasn't standard for a meat-packing facility.

Her curiosity piqued, Anna felt the familiar surge of adrenaline that came with the hunt.

Her mind shifted back to Tehran. Her back to a metal wall, much like this. Her target in the market square, drinking tea where he sat at a backgammon table, the scent of doner lingering on the air.

Two shots.

Both to the base of his skull.

It had been a message.

Her memories swirled, like tendrils of seaweed dragging at her, as if trying to pull her back into the depths, but she shrugged the thoughts aside. Determination settled in her bones like lead. She would find answers. She had to. The ghosts of her past operations whispered, her training a fuel reaching out through the years.

She crouched, observing. The guards moved with purpose but lacked the efficiency of military personnel. They followed a pattern—ten steps forward, a pause, a lazy turn, then back again. Predictable. Exploitable. Anna's mind catalogued their behavior, ticking off variables. A distraction was necessary, a diversion to draw them away from their post. She needed something loud, unexpected.

With a glance, she noted a stack of empty crates nearby. A simple push, the crash would echo through the steel and concrete like a gunshot. But timing was critical; too soon, and they'd be on her before she could move. Too late, and they'd see her.

Patience was part of the game. Her left hand, dominant and steady, hovered near her own weapon – a precaution. Every muscle coiled tight, she waited for the precise moment, for the guards' backs to turn one last time.

But a pause, and she noticed a switch near the crates.

Better.

Much better.

It might be attributed to a mechanical failure, and it would take longer to investigate.

She watched—the men's backs turned to her—then she reached out, flipping the metal switch.

The conveyor belt groaned to life. Metal clanged against metal, a cacophony in the stillness of the meat-packing plant. Anna pressed her body flat against the cold wall behind the towering crates, her breath steady. Eyes fixed on the guards, she watched shadows shift as they turned towards the noise.

"Check that out," one guard barked, voice sharp and slicing through the din. Steps quickened. Boots thudded against concrete floors, moving away.

Anna counted seconds, each one hanging heavy in the air. The guards' voices faded, swallowed by the sprawling factory. She slid from her hiding spot, eyes scanning the expanse before her. No movement. No sound but the persistent clatter of the belt. Time to move.

She moved with precision, steps measured and silent. A ghost slipping through an industrial maze. The path to the basement loomed ahead, a gaping mouth in the plant's underbelly. Darkness beckoned. She slipped inside, the chill of unseen walls grazing her skin. Her hand found a railing, cold and unyielding. Downwards, always downwards.

The basement air was stale. Anna's pulse thrummed in her ears, the only rhythm in the silence that enveloped her. Ahead, the faint outline of a door materialized from the shadows. She approached, senses alert, every nerve ending firing.

Safety off. Breathe out. Step forward. The descent continued.

The door creaked open, a soft groan in the silence. Anna paused, her hand on the knob, feeling the rust bite into her skin. The room beyond was a tomb of shadows, barely touched by the spill of dim light from the corridor. An old chair stood in the center of the room, its wood scarred and stained, the legacy of countless hours pressed into its grain.

Anna stepped inside, her boots soundless on the dusty floor. The air was thick with the musk of decay and the faintest trace of copper—blood long since dried to a memory. She approached the chair.

She knelt, left hand outstretched, fingertips grazing the rope fibers on the ground. They spoke of struggle, of desperation. Her eyes narrowed as she pieced together the story the silent witness tried to tell. Sammie's image flashed before her eyes—the young boy who vanished without a trace, leaving a town clutching at ghosts.

Standing, she scanned the room one last time; the walls seemed to lean in, hungry for the next secret to swallow.

Anna's eyes narrowed as she caught sight of the open doorway across the room. This one opposite to the door she'd entered through. Another passage, another question hanging in the stale air. She crossed the threshold, her boots whispering against the concrete floor. Each step was measured, a silent testament to her training. The path before her sloped upward into burgeoning sunlight, and she felt the familiar clench of caution in her gut.

Stairs ascended. Dust particles floated in the scant beams that penetrated the stairwell.

The wooden steps creaked under her weight, a sound that seemed too loud in the silence. Her left hand brushed the wall for balance, feeling the rough texture of aged brick. It crumbled slightly, the grit of it settling on her fingertips.

Anna emerged from the underbelly of the meat-packing plant, her boots grazing the top stair with practiced stealth. Before her stretched a dense copse of trees, their branches gnarled silhouettes against the darkening sky. Morning had begun to claim the landscape, wrapping everything in a cloak of shadows.

She scanned the ground. Leaves crunched lightly underfoot, each step deliberate, each breath measured. The foliage betrayed recent disturbances—footprints, both small and large, pressed into the earth. They wove between tree trunks and disappeared into the thicket. Someone had been here, and not long ago.

She knelt down, her left hand tracing the outline of the larger print.

A branch snapped.

"Freeze!"

The command cut through the silence like a bullet. Anna's body tensed. She spun, right hand rising, gun poised.

Two men. Guns trained on her. Their presence loomed from behind the rusted links of a fence that bordered the property. Faces hard. Eyes colder.

"Drop the weapon," the one on the left barked. His stance wide, his intention clear.

"Slowly," added the other, his finger hovering over the trigger with ominous ease.

Anna assessed. Calculated. Her eyes darted from muzzle to muzzle, gauging the distance, the risk, the chance of disarming and disabling before a shot could punctuate the standoff.

The chill in the air matched the ice in the men's stares. Sweat beaded on her brow, not from fear but from focus. She made a show of easing her grip on the gun, arm lowering by degrees until the pistol fell to the ground with a dull thud.

"Good choice," the left man growled. His weapon never wavered.

Anna's mind raced. Three tours. Countless encounters. This was familiar territory, yet each situation unique. A flicker of movement from her peripheral vision—a squirrel scampering across the smaller footprints. Evidence of Sammie's passing? No time to ponder.

"Step forward," the right man ordered. He motioned with his gun. "Against the fence."

The two men were inside the fence. She was outside. They wouldn't be able to reach her, but their bullets would have no such issue. Then again... now that the sun was rising, she could see the disrepair in the fence. Gaps a small child could have climbed through... or that an adult woman might reach through...

Anna took slow steps forward, each one deliberate. The morning air shivered the chain links between them, and Anna swayed a bit, approaching the men from an angle she preferred.

"Hands where we can see them." It was more than an order; it was a warning.

Anna complied. Left hand first. Then the right. Fingers splayed wide against the sky. Guns still pointed at her. Safety off. Their fingers itched for a reason.

"Who sent you?" the left man demanded. His voice was gravel, harsh and unyielding.

No answer from Anna. Silence sometimes spoke louder than words. She watched their eyes. Waited. Seconds stretched into eternity.

The right-hand man stepped forward. Impatience or bravery? A mistake.

"Answer!" he insisted.

A twig broke. A distraction. Not from Anna. A third party? Their heads turned. Fraction of a second. Opportunity.

Anna's hand shot forward.

And a gunshot echoed.

Chapter 7

The first guard never saw it coming. He'd allowed her to get too close, and now, Anna's hand snaked through the gap in the chain link, snatching at his gun hand with a violent jerk of his wrist. The gunshot echoed as the hot metal seared past Anna's shoulder.

She wrenched his arm forward as the bullet missed, moving to the right so the second guard had no clear line of fire. As the guard lost his grip on his pistol, Anna snatched it away, fluidly aiming at the second guard.

This second man was younger, with wide eyes and a frightened expression. He tried to aim for a clean shot, but his partner was in the way.

"Drop it," Anna commanded, her voice low and devoid of inflection. The second guard hesitated, his eyes darting between his companion's pained grimace and the barrel of Anna's gun.

She knew the outcome before it even occurred.

The younger man with the panicked look stammered once, twice, and then his fingers slackened. Metal kissed the ground with a dull thud.

"Down. Now." Her directive sliced through the air, leaving no room for dissent. The guards complied, their bodies meeting earth. Dust kicked up around them. She held the gun steady, unwavering.

Anna's breath came slow and controlled, her grip on the stolen gun unyielding. The air hung heavy with the scent of rusted metal and fear. Her eyes narrowed, scanning for movement beyond the downed guards.

"Where's Sammie?" she snapped, searching the factory behind them.

Neither of them spoke.

"You'd better surrender," snapped the man whose wrist she'd sprained. He was nursing his injured arm while eating turf. "If you know what's good for you. The boss is gonna mess you up."

"Yeah? And who's this boss?"

Anna breathed heavily, glancing one way, then the other.

Suddenly, both men—even from where they lay on the ground—stiffened. Their eyes widened as they stared past Anna.

For a moment, she thought it was a ruse.

No one could sneak up behind her without her hearing them. It hadn't happened in years.

But both the guards were gaping past her. One of them let out a leaking breath, and he gasped out, "She snuck up on us! I swear!"

"Wasn't our fault!" the second guard was saying, staring past her.

Anna frowned. Still no sounds behind her, but she felt a cold prickle up her spine.

What the hell was going on here?

She turned, ever so slowly.

And that's when she saw him.

A man stood behind her, near the fence where it curved closer to the trees. His own shadow was swallowed by the shadow of the leaves swaying above him, rocking back and forth with each breath of the early morning.

Worst of all, she recognized the man.

She was so taken off guard, that she hesitated, her gun trained on the two guards behind the fence rather than whirling towards this new arrival.

She felt as if she were staring at a ghost.

What the hell was he doing in Maine?

His outline was softened by the gentle morning light filtering through the leaves, casting a warm glow around him. His broad shoulders were relaxed, and a casual smile played on his lips, giving him an air of approachability that clashed sharply with the tension of the situation. His hands were tucked into his belt, thumbs hooked lightly in the loops of his worn jeans. The hems of his plaid shirt fluttered lightly in the breeze, creating a rhythmic rustling sound that seemed to harmonize with the swaying trees.

He looked more like a country boy than the head of security, with his cavalier attitude and his trademark smile, not to mention his suspenders and flannel shirt.

"Anna Gabriel, as I live and breathe," he said in a lazy drawl, his voice deep and smooth like velvet. "I guess some things never change, huh?"

Her heart pounded in her chest, and she felt her grip on the gun tighten. She didn't like being caught off guard.

"What are you doing here, Landon?" she demanded, narrowing her eyes and attempting to regain some control over the situation.

He shrugged, his thumbs still hooked casually in his belt loops, and said, "I'm working, Anna. And by the sound of things, you're making my job harder."

His accent was just like she remembered, as if he'd tried to hide it but had never quite been able to mask it completely.

Anna hesitated for a moment, her mind racing. She could feel her adrenaline pumping through her veins, a reminder that she was still on high alert.

Again, she was struck by the impossibility of it all.

Anna's eyes widened as she took in his appearance. The man looked like he belonged in a different world, far removed from the gritty reality of their current predicament. There was something disarming about his easy grin and the way he stood there, seemingly unaffected by the chaos surrounding them. His sandy-brown hair caught glimpses of sunlight, casting a halo around his head.

She couldn't help but feel a mix of disbelief and confusion at his sudden appearance. Landon had always been known for his calm demeanor and tactical prowess back when they were both in BUDS training together. Yet, seeing him here now, in this unexpected setting, raised more questions than answers.

Landon Byers. A ghost from a past she thought buried. His stride was steady, confident—unhurried. He stopped just outside the reach of her shadow. She froze. Not from fear. Surprise. His face was a roadmap of shared history, each line a memory.

"Anna," Byers said, his voice a smooth contrast to the gravel beneath his feet. "Mind telling me why you're busting up my operation?"

Anna's finger rested against the trigger, poised but still. The arm that held the gun did not tremble. It never did. His words were a riddle wrapped in the mundane, but danger hummed between them like a live wire.

"Why the hell are you here?" she snapped.

"Working a private security gig," Byers continued, hands casual at his sides, betraying nothing. "This place is one of our contracts."

"Private security?" Her voice was a whip-crack in the silence. "Or private army?"

Byers met her gaze, unflinching. "You know how it is. We go where the work is."

The two guards behind the fence were slowly rising, lulled by the singsong cadence of a southern gentleman turned gun-for-hire.

Unlike most members of the SEAL teams, Byers boasted no tattoos. But as the guards tried to rise, Anna reacted.

"Down. Now!" Anna's command sliced through the morning air, her voice edged with authority honed on foreign soil. The guards hesitated, their eyes flicking between her and Byers, weighing their odds.

"Get on the ground, or I drop you where you stand," she said, her grip on the stolen gun unwavering.

Byers said, congenially, "She's a good shot. Always been better than me. I'd listen if I were you."

The guards complied, hitting the dirt with grunts of resignation. Their remaining weapon lay discarded. They muttered protests, their words muffled against the ground.

Byers gestured to the guards, his motions deliberate, revealing nothing but calm professionalism. "They're just doing their job," he said, his tone even.

"Security," she said flatly, the word a bullet itself. "Is that what we're calling hired guns these days?"

"Anna—" Byers started, but she cut him off with a sharp wave of the gun.

"Save it. You've got five seconds to start making sense." Her voice was low, a growl almost, daring him to lie. "I saw the basement."

He frowned briefly. Byers held her gaze, his face a mask of professional regret. "We were brought in to handle a specific threat."

"Specific threat," Anna echoed, her suspicion a living thing. She remembered sniper drills, the echo of gunfire, the smell of cordite. She remembered trust, and how easily it could be betrayed.

"Got a problem with that?" Byers asked. His eyes held hers, steady, revealing nothing.

"Depends," Anna said. The word hung between them—a challenge. Her stance unyielding, she weighed every possible implication of his presence. Private security could mean protection. It could also mean a cleanup crew.

"Depends on what?" Byers tilted his head, a slight motion. Expectant.

"Your involvement." Anna's jaw tightened. Answers. She wanted answers. Needed them. The mayor's son. The mayor's death. Byers here, now, it wasn't coincidence. Couldn't be.

"Let's just say I'm here to ensure things run smoothly."

"Is that why you had a kid tied up in your basement?"

Byers shook his head. "Wasn't us."

"Bullshit."

"Wasn't. We got here just a couple hours before you."

"Why?"

"Looking for that same kid, Anna. Sammie. His mother wants him back."

"You're working for the mayor's wife?"

Byers didn't answer this. Instead, his thumbs still hooked in loops of fabric, he said, "Why don't you tell me why you're here, Anna. Bodies have been dropping, and lo and behold, I find the Guardian Angel herself down in Clearwater."

"What are the odds," she muttered.

"Not great."

"The mayor's son. The death of the mayor," she pressed, her words bullets loaded with the weight of suspicion and anger. "You're going to give me something, Byers, or this gets ugly."

Byers held her gaze, his eyes steady but not without a flicker — a flicker that spoke volumes to Anna. He inhaled slowly, buying time, choosing his words with the care of a man defusing a bomb. He had never been the sort to take a direct approach—not even on the teams.

He hadn't been lying when he'd said she'd always been a better shot than him. It was his one weakness. He didn't know how to hit the earth without the help of gravity.

But he was smart.

Far, far smarter than most—and tactically, there were few better. Still, he'd never been an ambitious sort. He preferred the role of second-in-command rather than first.

She suspected this was his way of avoiding responsibility. But another part of her wondered if he simply knew the game better than most.

"Things aren't as they seem," Byers said. His hands rose slightly, a gesture of peace or perhaps surrender. "You have to believe me. Why don't we sit down—discuss what we both know."

"How come you aren't surprised to see me here?"

"Casper," Byers said simply.

She scowled. "He gave me up."

"Nah. He just mentioned where you were heading."

"I didn't tell him."

Byers shrugged. "I mean... it's the Friendly Ghost. He keeps an eye on his friends."

"That's why you two are still talking? Friends?"

Byers shrugged. "Gotta get my work from someone. Now how about you tell me what you know about Sammie's kidnapping."

"I know he was in a basement back there, and I know your guys were guarding him."

"We weren't. Like I said, we only just arrived."

"I don't believe you."

Byers just shrugged, leaning against a tree now and watching her from under casual, hooded eyes.

Anna's eyes flicked to the edges of the compound, her instincts whispering warnings. Byers stood too still, too calm. The quiet buzz in the air—it wasn't just tension, it was expectation. Back-up. Her mind flashed through scenarios, each one ending with her cornered or worse. Time was a luxury slipping away.

"Anna?" Byers' voice held a note of caution, as if he sensed her shift in focus.

"Shut up," she hissed without looking at him. Every sense strained for the telltale crunch of boots on gravel, the static crackle of a radio about to spit out her location. She began to retreat, step by measured step, her gun unwavering from its target.

"You're stalling," she said suddenly.

The moment she spoke it, it was as if a spell were cast. A jeep appeared around the side of the packing plant. Men with guns bristled from in the cabin. A lot of them.

Shit.

She turned sharply.

"Anna, let's just sit down and chat. Get all our cards on the table. Better than either of us getting shot here, right?"

Anna ignored him, her gun now trained on her old military buddy. Her gaze sliced to the ground, sweeping over the dirt and debris. Footprints. Scattered, chaotic.

"You're making a mistake, Guardian. Let's talk this through—"

She cut him off with a sharp jab of the gun.

"Move again, and I shoot."

Stepping back, her back to the woods, the safety of shadows calling, Anna's fingers rested on the trigger, light but ready. She wouldn't hesitate if it came down to it. She never did. The jeep was rapidly approaching. A hundred yards away. Fifty.

"Anna—"

"Stay back," she warned. And with that, she turned, the woods swallowing her whole, leaving only the echo of her departure and the unanswered questions hanging thick in the air.

There just wasn't time. If Byers was telling the truth, then this was a complication she couldn't get caught in. If he was lying—She shook her head. It didn't matter. Either way, the trail was telling a story.

Sammie Henderson was out here.

Her eyes cast to the tracks on the ground, scanning the smallest ones.

Was Byers telling the truth? Had Sammie's mother hired him?

Bullshit. Byers had always been an excellent infiltrator; he wasn't a security guard. He worked conflict zones, countries where insurgents and rebellion were the daily fare. What the hell was he doing in Maine?

Thick underbrush snagged at Anna's boots. Each step was a calculated risk, one she was willing to take. The creek ahead gurgled, a soft sound but jarring in the quiet of the woods. She paused, her trained eyes scanning the ground. Footprints. Small. Too small for an adult. They pressed into the mud beside the water.

Shouts arose behind her, but no pursuing footsteps yet.

A good way to get oneself shot was to run pell-mell after a SEAL with no visual.

Anna crouched, her left hand steady as she traced the outline of a print with a finger. Child-sized. Vulnerable. Her mind cataloged the details: depth, direction, spacing. The mayor's son. Could these be his?

With her pulse thrumming a relentless beat, Anna stood and followed the trail. Trees loomed overhead, their branches like dark sentinels watching her every move.

The creek curved, and the footprints veered with it, leading away from the beaten path. Anna hesitated, then pushed forward. The darkness of the woods could hide anything—friend, foe, or truth. The unknown didn't deter her; it propelled her.

Anna's boots slipped on a slick patch of leaves, her hand shooting out to steady herself against a gnarled oak. No fall. No noise. She pressed on, the underbrush giving way beneath her determined strides.

What the hell was Byers doing in Maine? It was as if trouble kept finding her. Or as if she couldn't resist it, like a magnet drawn to metal.

She cursed bitterly under her breath, reminding herself to give Casper a quick kick in the balls.

Byers was here because of her. No doubt about it.

So why was he on some private security team? Why the charade?

Her head hurt trying to figure out what it all meant. The man dead back at the motel. The mayor dead. The mayor's son missing. And now Landon Byers in Maine, pretending to work for the mayor's wife...

Unless he really was working for her?

But why?

And how had both those men been murdered with no wounds and no sign of poisoning?

The thoughts continued to cycle rapidly.

The forest was dense here, the canopy a black shroud against the morning sky. Her eyes, accustomed to darkness after years in the field, scanned for disturbances, for signs of passage.

A snapped twig. Bent grass. Disturbed earth. Someone had come through here recently. Every sense taut, she advanced, gun at the ready, finger resting beside the trigger. Heartbeat steady. Breath even. A machine crafted for moments like this.

The ground rose, and with it, her pulse. She could almost feel the answers hovering just beyond reach, teasing her with their proximity. A clearing ahead. She approached, wary, the shadows morphing with each step.

"Come out," she whispered into the sunlight, not expecting an answer. The wind was her only reply, carrying the scent of pine and the promise of coming rain.

A rustle to her right. She pivoted, sighting down the barrel. Nothing there but a flurry of leaves caught in a sudden gust. She lowered the gun fractionally, her instincts screaming that time was slipping away.

Then, suddenly, a desperate shout.

A large figure emerged from behind a tree, swinging a branch like a club.

It would've cracked her skull, but she was no longer there.

One moment, standing still, the next ducking out of the way and using the large man's own momentum against him.

Anna spun around, gun at the ready, heart pounding in her chest. It wasn't Byers, but the man's face was twisted in fury, eyes burning with hatred. He lunged forward, his arms outstretched as if to wrap himself around her, but Anna was quicker. She slammed her foot down hard on his instep, doubling him over in agony.

Not wasting a breath, she swept his ankle with a practiced motion, sending him to the ground as his head whipped back, snapping against the soil with a sickening crunch.

Anna grimaced, pausing to watch her attacker's prone body.

He was still breathing, but unconscious. His eyes briefly fluttered sightlessly, his chest rising and falling, but he gave no signs of rousing anytime soon.

Sweeping her gaze around the woods, Anna looked to see if anyone else felt like crashing her investigation, but no other figures emerged. Not Byers or his men or even an errant deer.

No further threats.

Anna looked at the man more closely now. He was sweaty, breathing heavily. She guessed he'd been in the woods awhile. Her eyes trailing to the big man's feet, she pursed her lips as she tried to imagine if those feet had made the large prints she'd spotted, chasing Sammie's.

"Sammie?" she called into the trees. "Sammie, are you there?"

She glanced one way, then the other. No sign. But no sign of further tracks either.

Why had the big guy been crouched behind this tree? She stared at the large oak, blinked, and then slowly, her eyes moved up.

Leaves fluttered down, and she blinked. A small shadow sat on one of the highest branches, trembling. Two eyes blinked down at her, staring like an owl perched in the dark.

"Sammie?" she said.

The boy in the tree winced at his name and flung a stick at her. He missed.

Anna felt mix of sudden relief and urgency, holding up both hands. "Sammie, I'm here to help you."

He didn't speak. He swallowed, shaking his head hurriedly. His eyes were red-ringed.

She felt a flicker of pride, though she didn't even know the child. But he couldn't have been much older than ten, and he'd escaped that basement, climbed the tree... and even now, he was defiant.

Her type of kid.

"Look, if you stay up there, more bad men are gonna come. Men with guns. Got it?" She pointed to the man on the ground. "I stopped him from hurting you. You can trust me."

But Sammie didn't seem to believe her.

Anna felt frustrated, but she didn't choose to show it. What would Beth have done in a situation like this? Tender, gentle, kind Beth. What might she have done?

She thought she could hear movement through the trees again. Were the gunmen getting closer?

She took a step back to show she wasn't a threat, her gun hanging by her side. "Sammie, I need you to come down. It's not safe up there." Her voice was calm, kind. She saw a flicker of uncertainty in the boy's eyes.

The child shifted on the branch, his small hands clutching at the rough bark. Fear and wariness danced in his gaze, but something else too—a glimmer of hope, of longing for safety.

Anna lowered herself to one knee, keeping her eyes on his. "I promise I won't let anyone hurt you. But we need to get out of here before more bad men come looking for you."

Sammie hesitated, looking down at her with a mix of fear and indecision. For a moment, the forest was quiet around them, only the whisper of the wind through the leaves breaking the stillness.

He glanced at her, then at the man who'd been chasing him, then back at her again.

Then, shouts broke through the woods. Not far away. Birds took to flight above the branches, sending small twigs scattering, their wings flapping on the sun-kissed breeze. Then, slowly, like a delicate bird leaving its nest for the first time, Sammie began to descend from the tree. His movements were cautious, his eyes never leaving Anna's face.

When he finally reached the ground, he stood before her, small and vulnerable in the vastness of the woods. Anna saw a tear slip down his cheek, leaving a trail through the dirt smudged on his face.

She reached out a hand, hesitated for just a moment before gently resting it on his shoulder. "It's going to be okay now," she said softly. "Let's get you somewhere safe."

Sammie nodded, his trust in her growing by fractions, but as Anna reached out her hand, he didn't take hold, preferring to ball his fingers into little fists, ready at his side.

Anna lowered her hand, then held a finger to her lips. "We need to be quiet. Come—this way. They won't find us if you follow my lead."

Sammie still looked hesitant. The shouts of the gunmen were growing closer now, pushing Anna to move swiftly. She gestured for Sammie to follow her silently as she led the way deeper into the forest. The shadows of the towering trees enveloped them like a protective cloak, muffling their movements.

Every rustle, every crack of a branch underfoot made both of them freeze momentarily, their senses heightened.

It wasn't until they'd reached the creek she'd spotted earlier that Anna whispered, "We need to run now."

Sammie just shook his head. He pointed. She glanced down at his feet, then winced.

Barefoot. Both of his feet were bleeding, rubbed raw from the detritus. He hadn't made a sound about it until now.

She wondered how much pain he was in.

"Okay, okay, that's okay... On my back, okay? I'll carry you."

Part of her wanted to lie. To say his mother had sent her, but she couldn't bring herself to fib. Not even for a good cause.

Instead, she extended a hand in offering once more. To her surprise, Sammie looked almost relieved. She noticed he was limping now on those bloody feet as he hobbled over to her, and once he reached her, she carefully took his weight on her back. He clung onto her neck, his small arms wrapping tight around. She adjusted her grip on his tiny limbs, her eyes scanning the thick woods.

"Hold on tight," she whispered. "We'll get you back to your mom."

Suddenly Anna was fighting for balance as Sammie's little fists came down on her back and his bloody feet kicked at her kidneys, fighting as he desperately tried to throw himself into the little river.

Chapter 8

Anna's steps were measured, each footfall a soft thud on the worn carpet of the RV. She moved back and forth like a caged animal, her brow furrowed deep with concern.

"We have to take him back," Anna said, pausing to glance at the small boy who sat huddled on the dinette bench. His eyes were wide, his body rigid with an unspoken fear. "Sammie," she continued, softer this time, "your mom—"

He shook his head, violently, locks of hair flinging side to side. His small hands gripped the edge of the table, knuckles white. No words came from his mouth, but his message was clear as day: he wouldn't go.

Though she'd managed to get him safely back, twice now he'd reacted this way at the mention of his mother.

Beth moved closer to Sammie, her presence a stark contrast to the tension that Anna carried. She kneeled down, bringing herself to his eye level, and reached out with a gentle hand that settled on his shoulder.

"Hey, it's okay," Beth murmured, her voice a soothing balm. "Everything is going to be alright." Her tone held a promise, one she aimed to keep.

Anna watched, her arms crossed now, as Beth's calm washed over the boy. There was something ethereal about the way she connected with children, a skill Anna acknowledged but didn't possess. Maybe it was the patience she exuded or the unwavering kindness in her eyes. Anna knew how to end life with precision, but Beth, she could mend spirits just as expertly.

And there was something else in her sister's eyes. Something that threatened to break Anna's heart—some sort of... longing in her gaze. Anna had heard Beth in her sleep back in the motel, murmuring the names of her children. Tony... Sarah...

Anna felt a pang lance through her heart; an odd sort of pain. Not the sort of wound one could mend on the field of battle using gauze and sutures. It was a sort of pain she was helpless to do anything about.

Anna had agreed to stay in Clearwater at her sister's request. But now, watching Beth with Sammie... Anna almost felt as if this was far more healing than anything Anna had done so far. She felt a lump form in her throat and frowned again.

It was the lack of sleep, she decided. She swallowed, pacing again. Her brow furrowed as her mind wandered beyond the walls of the RV they'd parked near the lake in an empty lot.

The forest preserve was closing soon, and they'd have to leave then before park rangers showed up, but for now, she was grateful for the privacy.

They needed time to think.

To figure out their next move.

But Sammie... he was acting oddly. It didn't make sense. Why wouldn't the child want to return home.

It didn't help that he seemed to be mute. He either couldn't speak or didn't want to.

"Trust us, Sammie," Beth continued, her assurance steady. "I won't let anyone hurt you. I promise."

The boy looked up at Beth, his expression a tangle of hope and fear. Anna felt the weight of responsibility press down on her shoulders, heavier with each passing second. The world outside the RV was a battlefield of different sorts, one where a young, innocent life like Sammie's could be easily caught in the crossfire.

But why didn't he want to return home? That seemed like the first step in unraveling all of this.

Anna knelt in front of Sammie, her eyes level with his. He swallowed briefly, looking more nervous as his gaze turned from Beth to Anna. The RV's interior was cramped, the air thick with tension. She could see the boy's chest rising and falling rapidly, his small hands fidgeting in his lap.

"Sammie," she began, voice low, "did your mom have anything to do with your father's death?"

Time hung suspended. Outside, leaves rustled against the window, an unwelcome intrusion. Sammie's mouth opened, then closed. A nod, slow, almost imperceptible, but it was there. Anna's heart thumped louder, a drumbeat echoing in the confined space.

"Okay." Anna took a breath, steadied herself. "Did you see your mother murd—"

"Anna!" Beth said sharply.

Anna grimaced and adjusted the question as Sammie stared at her, wide-eyed and horrified. "Did you see your mother hurt your father?"

Sammie hesitated, and swallowed, glancing nervously at the RV door.

"It's alright," Beth encouraged.

Sammie shook his head.

"Are you sure?" Anna asked.

"Maybe he didn't *see* it," Beth said, emphasizing the word.

Anna's gaze pinned the boy to his seat. "Sammie, did she do it? Was she behind your father's death?"

Beth was still frowning, disapproving, but Anna pressed on. If they were going to help Sammie, she needed to know what they were up against. Protecting Beth meant staying near. And Beth wanted to protect Sammie.

There was no option for her.

His small frame shrunk away from her, a slight tremor in his shoulders. He shook his head, lips pressed into a thin line. No words, just a silent negation carrying the weight of a child's confusion and fear.

A sigh escaped Anna's lips, her jaw tight. She glanced at Beth, who stood by the counter, eyes on Sammie, hand absentmindedly adjusting the volume knob on the TV. The murmurs of a news anchor bled into the room, an incessant hum that Anna barely registered.

She paced the narrow aisle of the RV. Three steps forward. Turn. Three steps back. Her movements were precise, betraying her military discipline.

Clearwater. A small town with big secrets now thrust into the spotlight. And here they were, harboring a child with answers locked inside him like a coded message.

"Damn it," she muttered under her breath. Clearwater couldn't handle this attention; the scrutiny would be relentless.

The FBI lurked at the edge of her subconscious. Always out there... Always a threat.

All the while they talked to Sammie, Beth continued to hover near the television, casting worried glances at the rescued child and then at Anna. The low drone of the broadcast at least offered some white noise if not comfort.

Suddenly Sammie's arm shot out. His child-sized finger jabbed toward the television screen. He made a gesture which Beth interpreted.

"You... want to listen?"

Sammie nodded hurriedly. Beth responded to the urgency in his gesture, her own hand reaching out to comply. The volume rose, slicing through the silence.

"–and we are all deeply saddened by the loss of our beloved Mayor," came the solemn voice of the news presenter from the TV speakers. His expression grave, his tone heavy with sorrow.

Anna ceased pacing and turned sharply towards the noise. Her gaze locked onto Sammie, who sat stiffly on the small bench, his eyes fixed on the screen. There was no mistaking the intensity in the boy's stare, the hard set of his small jaw.

But he wasn't staring at the TV presenter. Rather, his eyes were fixated on the man in the background where he stood giving some speech outside an official looking building.

The television presenter narrated. "Earlier today, Alfred Harrington, of Harrington Pharmaceuticals, issued a statement about his grief over the death of the mayor..." The presenter continued to drone on, but Anna and Beth were both watching their mute witnesses' gaze.

Sammie looked downright furious. He was shaking his head angrily side to side.

"You okay there, buddy?" Beth asked softly.

Sammie just frowned at the image of Alfred Harrington, and Beth eventually turned off the TV, casting them all in silence once more.

Anna studied Sammie's face as he stared at his hands where he sat on the bench.

Maybe Sammie's mother hadn't killed the mayor...

Anna nodded thoughtfully. What sort of mother would kill a boy's father in front of him? But Sammie somehow knew his mother was involved. So, she focused back on Sammie. "Do you know someone named Landon Byers?"

Sammie's eyes, wide and searching, met hers. He shook his head. No recognition. A dead end, just like that. Not that Anna had expected the former SEAL to introduce himself by name to his kidnappee—even if Landon was as involved as she still suspected.

"Alright." Anna stood up. She turned to Beth, who watched from the makeshift kitchenette, her face etched with concern.

"Keep him safe," Anna said, more command than request, and Beth nodded, understanding the weight of the instruction.

"Where are you going?"

"To get some answers."

Anna locked the RV door behind her, the click of the mechanism a sharp punctuation in the dusk. Gravel crunched underfoot as she strode away from the vehicle. Behind her, the faint glow of interior lights leaked out, casting long shadows on the ground.

She heard the window sliding, and she glanced back, frowning to see her sister's face framed.

"Where exactly are you headed?" Beth's voice came through the half-open window, tinted with concern.

"The coroner's office," Anna replied without turning. Her words cut the distance between them, clear and purposeful. "I need to see the reports, the actual causes of death. There might be something there."

Beth nodded inside the RV, her silhouette framed against the dimness. "And if there is?"

"Then we'll know what we're dealing with." Anna paused, her hand hovering over her weapon, a cold comfort at her side. She scanned the horizon, the town's sparse lights winking like distant stars. "Stay alert, Beth. Keep him safe."

Chapter 9

Landon Byers plucked another ruby seed from the open pomegranate. The juice stained his fingertips as he brought it to his mouth, the tartness a sharp contrast to the air heavy with old leather and ink. His eyes, dark and focused, observed the burst of crimson against his pale skin before he crushed the seed between his teeth.

The door to the study slammed open with an urgency that sent a shiver through the room, but Landon didn't react. He didn't so much as glance over, preferring to pluck another red seed and toss it into his mouth. He leaned idly against an old, worn bookcase which he guessed was worth more than he'd made in two tours, and that included med-comp for the bullet lodged in his ribs on his right side. A memento of a bygone era.

Being shot gave someone perspective.

And now, a figure loomed, all anger and indignation, draped in red velvet that whispered power and a taste for theatrics. The older man's face flushed a matching shade as he barreled into the space, his presence filling the room with a different kind of weight.

"Byers!" His voice cracked like a whip, each syllable a demand, a rebuke. "How did you let her slip through? Who is she?"

Landon selected another pomegranate seed, deliberate, unhurried. The older man's hands balled into fists, the fabric of his suit straining at the seams. Landon's jaw worked methodically, the sound of the seed's destruction a quiet counterpoint to the older man's heavy breathing.

As the older man advanced, a storm of scarlet and silver hair, his shadow fell over Landon. "I'm waiting for an explanation, Byers." The velvet-clad figure loomed closer, his voice less thunderous now but edged with steel.

Landon plucked another seed. Red juice beaded on his fingertip. He placed it in his mouth, the sound crisp in the silence that followed the question. No flinch. No furrowed brow. Just the meticulous dismantling of a fruit, seed by seed.

"Damn it! Look me in the eyes. We had a deal," the older man snapped.

"I know." Landon's voice was flat, almost bereft of concern.

"Damn it, Landon." Fingers grazed the polished wood of an antique globe, the older man's attempt to channel his frenzy into motion. But the globe spun silently, continents blurring. "Who was she?"

"She's nobody," Landon said simply. "Wrong place, wrong time. She's lost in the woods."

"Nobody? I heard she disarmed two of your men."

"Nu-uh. Not my men."

"Men under your supervision, though," the man in the red suit said as if playing a trump card.

Landon shrugged. "I took the job in good faith. I'll finish the job. But what did you want me to do? Shoot her?"

"She *was* trespassing," growled the older man.

He looked weary now. Landon had taken the job on short notice, two weeks before. Ever since talking with Casper and being directed to Anna Gabriel's next pit stop. He'd waited in Clearwater, Maine. Watching for signs of her. But Guardian Angel was just as careful as she'd ever been. He smirked a little at that. He'd been looking for her, patiently watching. Then without setting off any of his feelers, she'd run barrel-first into him in at the plant.

Call it luck. Call it Kismet.

Either way, now she was here. But she couldn't know he'd come to find her. Not yet. Not until... he had his ducks in a row.

Landon gave a soft smile, wiping the back of his hand across his lips.

The older man's breath slowed. His gaze dropped from Landon to the bookcases lining the walls, each shelf groaning under the weight of leather-bound secrets and gilt-edged histories. He inhaled slowly, exhaled, as if steeling himself. Finally, after what felt like an eternity, he spoke.

"Hawaiian koa," the silver-haired man muttered, almost to himself. The words came out soft and prayerful as a confession. "Rare wood. Expensive. Like everything else in this room."

Landon glanced up, just for a moment. His fingers pinched another crimson seed. He placed it between his lips and nodded toward the older man—an acknowledgment of the statement and nothing more.

"Craftsmanship," the older man continued, tracing the grain of the wood with a finger, as if these details could anchor him, pull him back from the brink. "They don't make them like this anymore."

Landon's expression remained unreadable. No trace of judgement. No sign of approval.

The older man's shoulders slumped, the energy of his anger dissipating like mist in sunlight. He staggered backward, the fury that had once propped him up now abandoning him to gravity's pull. With a final, feeble step, he fell into the leather chair behind him. It groaned under his weight, a sound that echoed off the book-laden walls. His chest heaved. Once. Twice. Then settled into the rhythm of defeat.

Landon's fingers paused mid-air, a single pomegranate seed pinched between them. He turned his head slowly towards the older man, his eyes betraying none of the calm that coated his voice. "I know who she is."

The older man looked up, his face a landscape of lines etched by years and stress. "You do?" His voice cracked, a note of hope threading through the exhaustion.

"Yes." Landon dropped the seed into his mouth, the sound sharp in the silence.

"Who is she?" The older man's voice was a strained whisper, barely lifting above the weight of his own breath.

He didn't rush to answer, allowing the question to hang in the air as if it were as inconsequential as the dust motes dancing in the shafts of light from the window.

"The woman I came for," Landon said at last, his eyes fixed on the older man, steady and unblinking.

"From Maine?" The older man leaned forward.

"Passing through." Landon's words were crisp.

"Is my money not enough? Is that why you let her go?" Suspicion laced the older man's tone now, a new thread of concern weaving through the fabric of his exhaustion.

A smile tugged at the corner of Landon's mouth, but it didn't reach his eyes. He winked, a flicker of something unreadable passing over his face. "I'll get the job done. I need the cash."

The older man nodded slowly, the lines in his forehead deepening with the motion.

"She has nothing to do with this. Any of it," Landon said simply. "She won't be a problem again."

The older man's fingers drummed on the arm of his chair, his agitation clear despite the slump of his shoulders. He eyed Landon.

"Who is she to you?"

"Nobody to concern yourself about," he said. "She's no threat. At least not to you."

"Then why—" The older man started, but Landon held up a hand, silencing him.

His gaze locked onto something unseen, a momentary shift to steel behind his calm exterior. "Who was in that basement, sir... I didn't agree to protect a kidnapped kid."

Landon said his piece quietly, deliberately. He didn't hesitate the moment he began to speak, and once he'd finished, he went quiet, waiting.

The old man hesitated, blinking. He had a good poker face and hid his reaction as quickly as it threatened to come.

Landon could feel his irritation. He'd taken the job—a protection gig. Nothing more. And no one had said anything about kidnapped kids. Things were quickly getting out of hand.

A pause hung between them, weighted. The older man's eyes narrowed, his lips pressed into a thin line. He leaned back, his body language closing off as if bracing against an invisible storm.

"Does it concern you?" His voice was a low rumble, defensive walls rising.

Landon's jaw clenched, a subtle sign of resolve.

The older man's hand ceased its rhythmic drumming and pointed a stiff finger at Landon. "You're here to follow my orders. Not to question them. I had the impression you were a professional."

Landon set aside the pilfered pomegranate, its flesh now a hollowed husk. He met the older man's glare with unwavering eyes. "Information is security. Your safety depends on it."

"Is that so?" The older man scoffed, but his voice cracked like thin ice underfoot.

"Without honesty, I'm blind in the dark. And you," Landon said, leaning forward, "are out in the open."

The room went still. The tension hung between them, a silent standoff in the midst of opulence. Then, the older man's posture wilted, his resistance crumbling like dry earth. His eyes slid from the defiant face before him to the plush carpet beneath his feet.

"Fine," he murmured. "The mayor... he's been found dead."

Landon's expression did not change. "I know that. Everyone knows that."

"Yes... but you're not listening, are you?"

"What does that have to do with a boy in the basement?"

"I didn't say there was any boy."

"Are you denying it?"

"Categorically. Do your job, Landon. Let me do mine."

"And this has to do with the mayor, how, exactly?"

"Murdered," the older man murmured to himself, his fingers now tracing patterns on the leather of his chair. "Which means they could be coming for me next."

"Who are 'they'?" Landon asked, every muscle taut, ready to spring into action if needed.

"I am paying you so handsomely," the older man whispered, "because that is a question I hope to never see an answer for." Rubbing his nose, the grey-haired man let out a sigh. "Men like me... we close our eyes and see a hundred silhouettes. Vague shadows holding daggers meant for us. You want to know who is coming for me? A lifetime of making enemies is coming for me. I don't know which hand holds the dagger, but I assure you there *is* a dagger for me. Now. Is that enough context for you to do the job I've hired you for?"

Landon shrugged once, tossing his fruit husk into the trashcan at the side of the large table. "I'll handle it," Landon stated, his voice firm, devoid of doubt.

A pause hung in the air, thick with unspoken fears. The older man's hand trembled ever so slightly, betraying his stoic facade.

"Keep me safe, Byers," he implored, a rare crack in his authoritative tone.

"No kids," Landon said simply.

His would-be boss just frowned.

Landon winked—a solitary motion, swift and sure. The older man's gaze followed Landon as he strode across the study, each step deliberate.

At the door, Landon paused but did not turn. "Lock this down after I leave," he instructed, pointing to the heavy mahogany door. "Double the guards."

The older man nodded, his head a slow pendulum of compliance.

With one last glance at the bookcases, Landon stepped out into the corridor. The click of the closing door severed the connection between them.

Landon had taken the job. He needed the money.

But he was in Maine for one reason alone.

And that reason had a name: Anna Gabriel.

Chapter 10

The rear window clacked back into its frame from where she'd pried it open with the edge of the compact karambit knife she kept for these special occasions.

Anna slipped into the coroner's office, glancing over her shoulder towards the nearly abandoned parking lot.

She'd waited until the darkness had come in completely. It was one thing she'd always been good at: waiting patiently. How many times, as a sniper, had she been in an uncomfortably itchy ghillie suit while waiting in the cold or wet. Once, she'd been so still, so camouflaged, that a mountain goat had started eating pieces off her ghillie suit.

Waiting, sitting still, motionless, with no entertainment, nothing to distract herself but her own thoughts—this was an uncommon skill.

But that wasn't to say she wasn't glad it was over.

Now, letting the window close behind her, she dusted some of the bark residue off her hand from where she'd used it to lean against the large oak tree in the park two streets down.

The last of the cop cars had passed nearly two hours ago.

Anna's shadow merged with the darkness as she edged along the sterile white corridor of the coroner's office. The muted hum of fluorescent lights overhead was the only sound betraying the late hour, as she paused to let the pulse of adrenaline settle into a steady thrum in her veins.

The door to the coroner's inner sanctum loomed before her. She pushed it open softly.

Inside, the air held a chill that seeped into her bones. Anna's eyes scanned the room, darting from one corner to the next as she navigated the space with silent precision. The room was sterile, filled with stainless steel tables and cabinets housing various tools and equipment, and a faint scent of antiseptic lingered in the air, mixing with the metallic tang of blood.

Anna's gaze landed on a row of stainless-steel fridge compartments along one wall. She knew what she was looking for—the body of the mayor. She moved swiftly and noiselessly towards the fridges, her heart pounding in her chest. As she reached for the handle of one of the compartments, a sudden sound made her freeze.

Footsteps.

Anna's breath caught in her throat as she spun around, searching for a place to hide. But just as quickly as the sound arrived, it passed.

A late-night worker, then. Or a guard, going about their rounds?

She shook her head, releasing a slow breath of relief.

In the corner, an oversized compartment drew her attention—a chart resting against it, sealed with a lock. This had to be it: the resting place of the city's beloved figurehead. Her heart quickened, not with fear but with purpose.

The lock was a simple tumbler mechanism, nothing that would challenge her skills honed in more perilous theatres. Anna crouched, her left hand steady as she extracted a slim lock pick from the inner recesses of her jacket. The metal tool felt cold, familiar against her fingertips. She inserted it into the keyhole, angling it just so, applying subtle pressure. Her right hand followed with a torsion wrench, seeking the quiet click of pins falling into place.

Time ticked away in soft, muted thuds of her heartbeat. Eyes narrowed, she listened to the faint scrape of metal on metal, her focus unwavering. Within moments, the satisfying turn of the cylinder signaled success. But before she could pull the heavy latch, the distant sound of footsteps echoed through the cold, inhospitable corridors, approaching.

Returning.

Shit.

She stiffened, staring towards the door.

And it began to open.

Shit.

She had to hide. Now.

She could hear voices. Not just one, then. Multiple threats.

There was nowhere to hide in the coroner's office. The cupboards were small. One across the room was locked but wouldn't have helped anyway as it had a glass window.

Her eyes narrowed in sudden cold focus as Anna glanced analytically across the room, searching swiftly for a place to conceal herself.

The fridge compartments.

Steeling herself, she hurriedly slipped one out, jumping headfirst into the open slot in the same motion.

Shit. It already had a body housed inside.

Anna grimaced in frustration, her mind flashing back to another scene—similar. She'd hidden among the dead then, but their corpses had been far fresher and warmer. Still, if the choices were between discovery and discomfort, you made your peace and apologized to the ghosts later.

The stench of formaldehyde invaded her senses as she pressed herself against the back wall of the compartment, her heart pounding in her ears. Anna's breaths came in short, controlled bursts, pulling the slab door as closed as she dared, straining to listen to the approaching footsteps and squinting into the narrow slit of light showing the room beyond.

The door to the room swung open with a soft creak, and through the small slit, Anna could see the figure of the coroner—judging by his white lab coat—appear.

She grimaced resolutely. While Anna wished she could simply close the hatch door until the coroner left, she couldn't shut it completely. Each body storage drawer had a latch, and it would only open from the outside. And if she locked herself in here...

Burying the thought, Anna hooked her foot on the inside lip of the morgue drawer and pulled the storage door a few centimeters more with her heel, plunging her world into further darkness.

Silence enveloped her, save for the shuffling of feet outside her temporary sanctuary. Anna's pulse thrummed in her ears, each beat a drum of warning. She stilled her breathing, muscles tensed for action yet forced into stillness. The space around her was close, frigid air clinging to her skin. A hint of chemical cleaner lingered, mixed with the faint, unmistakable scent of death.

The footsteps stopped just shy of her hiding spot. She imagined the intruder standing there, unknowingly inches away from discovery. Her fingers curled into her palm, ready to unleash trained violence if necessary. But no blow came. Only the slow, deliberate sounds of someone else at work, oblivious to the predator concealed in their midst.

Anna listened as the coroner moved about the room, the sounds of his work methodical and precise: a drawer slid open, instruments clinked, papers rustled. Each noise was magnified in the compact darkness where Anna lay in wait. Her eyes, adjusting to the absence of light, caught slivers of movement through the narrow cracks around the compartment door.

She watched. A vial placed on a counter. Hands—steady, practiced—scribbling notes. He was routine, methodical; his movements betrayed no knowledge of the intruder sharing his space.

Who had he been speaking to?

Himself?

She hesitated, frowning.

Minutes dragged. Anna's body ached from the chill morgue atmosphere and the forced stillness, but her mind was alert. She counted breaths, measured the time between the coroner's steps. Predictable patterns. Safe for now.

A new voice entered the room.

Anna frowned, listening, and a cold shiver went down her spine that had nothing to do with the refrigerated temperatures.

She recognized that voice. But from where?

"We're still looking into cause of death. You say you found something?"

She heard the swish of movement and imagined the coroner turning. Shadows moved around the gap of the fridge door. The stench of chemicals from the corpse beneath her lingered in her nose, and Anna readjusted, her hand touching the icy metal interior of the morgue drawer. She grimaced, shifting her posture again.

It almost looked as if she were doing a pushup, the body directly under her trim frame as she avoided contact as best she could, awkwardly looking back through the thin sliver of light into the autopsy room behind her.

But now, the coroner was replying. "What's an FBI agent from the other side of the country doing here anyway?"

"We think we have tabs on the killer... they left bodies behind them in Mammoth Lakes and Las Vegas as well..."

Anna froze. Shit.

Now she knew where she recognized the voice from.

She leaned forward, maneuvering quietly, squinting through the dark to the gap in the fridge door near her heel.

As her skin prickled from the chill, she found herself staring at a scowling, dark-skinned woman in a charcoal gray suit. The woman was tall, even taller than the coroner, and her head was shaved. Two simple orb earrings, silver, adorned her ears.

Agent Jefferson.

No sign of her partner, Greeves. But back in Mammoth Lakes, Jefferson had been the first person to suspect Anna of killing another agent—Agent Jefferson's fiancé.

Anna had taken down the bad guys who'd actually killed Jefferson's fiancé, but she hadn't exactly stuck around to help the FBI connect the dots. Who knew if Jefferson bought her side of the story, or if she still believed Anna had played a role in her fiancé's death. Either way, the whole series of events, not to mention the numerous human traffickers gunned down on Abdo Sahid's racetrack by a 'mysterious vigilante', had left a bad taste in the FBI's mouth. Anna knew she'd be in their files, a person wanted for further questioning if nothing worse.

But judging by this cross-country trip, the FBI was far closer to her than she'd first thought.

Shit. Had they somehow tracked her RV?

Possibly.

Anna ground her teeth in silence, a puff of misting breath slipping between her lips. She was loath to relinquish her mobile home. Still... if the Feds were somehow using it to track her.

She controlled her breathing, slinking further back into the shadows of the refrigerated compartment, her mind racing with the implications of Jefferson's presence in Clearwater. If she was here, that meant the FBI had some inkling of Anna's whereabouts or activities. Anna's jaw clenched at the realization that staying in this town was no longer an option.

But Beth wouldn't leave.

Not until Sammie was safe again—she was taking it as her own personal crusade.

Anna let out a slow breath.

"Thanks for meeting up, Dr. Keller," Jefferson's voice cut through the room, businesslike.

"Agent," the coroner acknowledged without looking up. "Didn't expect you this late."

"Neither did I," Jefferson replied. "But your message said you'd found something."

Anna couldn't see them from her metal-walled prison, but their proximity was palpable. Her own breath sounded too loud in her ears, her heartbeat a drum threatening to betray her. Every instinct screamed to flee, to fight, but logic held her in check. Wait. Listen. Survive.

And then, with the suddenness of a bullet, silence fell. The coroner had paused, perhaps sensing an imbalance in his domain. Anna held her breath, willing herself to become part of the sterile chill that surrounded her. Invisible. Undetectable.

The quiet stretched on, the tension in the room building like static before a storm. Then footsteps, a shuffle of papers, and the coroner replied. "I found this in the mayor's arm."

"Cause of death?"

"Hard to say. There are no toxins. No residual poison."

"So what is it? Just looks like a pill."

"It's not. Not a traditional one anyway. See this opening in its side? It is a small metal receptacle of some sort."

"And it was in his arm?"

"Mhmm. The item was inserted here," the coroner's voice broke through, clinical and detached. "Then... it looks as if it might have been triggered remotely."

"Triggered? To do what."

"I don't know yet... but cause of death is beginning to look like a pulmonary embolism. That's a blockage in one of the pulmonary arteries in your lungs, typically caused by blood clots that travel—"

"I'm aware of what an embolism is," Jefferson interjected. "But that seems like an unreliable way to murder someone. You're sure this device is what triggered it?"

The coroner paused, and Anna heard a long-suffering sigh. "Am I certain? No. But sudden large embolisms have a high mortality rate," the coroner explained. "And I find the idea of a man with no other risk factors or family history dying of an embolism *while* coincidentally carrying this strange device under his skin... well, *unlikely* is too gentle a word for what I think."

Anna's mind raced with this new information. A small metal object triggered remotely to cause a fatal embolism?

"How could this pill thing cause that?"

"My guess? An air bubble, or some expandible clotting medium, delivered directly into the bloodstream."

"So someone planted this... metal pill. How long has it been in his arm?"

"Judging by scarring, I'd say at least five years."

A low whistle from Jefferson. "What are you up to, Ms. Gabriel?"

Anna grimaced at the mention of her name. She scowled at the closed door. Jefferson was obsessed. Five years ago, Anna was in the middle of being court-martialed. She certainly wasn't in Clearwater, Maine, embedding a metal device into the mayor's arm, just to return five years later and trigger it.

But it left the question... who had done so?

Was that what had killed the hitman by the lake as well? Had someone triggered a similar device? And why?

She fidgeted uncomfortably, her arms beginning to shiver as her body fought the chill wrapping its numbing fingers around her joints and tendons.

Did the mayor know he had that item in his arm? Some sort of underworld insurance policy for his cooperation? There were so many questions. And so few answers.

"Any prints?" Jefferson's voice was sharp, a scalpel cutting through the silence.

"None. It's far too small to carry a useful print. And after the time it spent in the Mayor's body, I'm certain the only DNA to be found would be his," The coroner replied in his clinical, matter-of-fact tone.

"Contents?" There was a rustle of fabric, probably Jefferson shifting weight from one foot to another.

"Still analyzing. But it's sophisticated. Not your standard delivery."

Sophisticated. The word echoed in the cramped space, rattling against Anna's skull. Her fingers twitched involuntarily. Left hand clenching, the familiar ache for a weapon surged and subsided. No room for mistakes.

"Keep me posted on the analysis. We need to know what was in that tube." Jefferson's command sliced through the air, edged with authority. "I can't believe someone would go to all this trouble just for the hope that a small air bubble in the blood would take him out."

"Will do," the coroner assured, his voice receding into the background hum of machinery and soft beeps of monitors.

Anna's mind raced alongside her pounding heart. Despite their differences, she had to agree with Jefferson. The metal tube's purpose was key. A lethal device triggered from afar... but who planted it? And who else knew? Why the mayor?

She needed answers. But first, she needed out.

The chill of the fridge compartment had seeped into Anna's bones. Her breath, a controlled whisper against the stainless steel encasing her was a testament to her SEAL training. No chattering, no crazed spasming shivers. Stillness as her body internally fought to keep her muscles warm. A bead of sweat trailed down her temple, defying the cold, and she focused on the murmurs outside her metallic hideaway.

"Agent Jefferson," the coroner's voice, cautious, "who is this woman you suspect of being involved? Is she really a serial killer?"

"Let me put it this way, we suspect she killed seventeen men at a racetrack in Las Vegas—by herself. And she's also involved in the deaths of two FBI agents."

"Seventeen men?" The coroner let out a low whistle, though he sounded quietly incredulous. Anna could almost picture the look of clinical disbelief on his face.

"From what we gathered, she's a sniper," Jefferson continued, her voice cold. "She likes killing from a distance. So this... this fits her MO."

A shiver ran down Anna's spine. Conveniently, in her outrageous accusations, Agent Jefferson had neglected to mention the men at the racetrack were *armed* and holding several kidnapped women hostage. However, despite her obvious bias, Anna knew better than to underestimate Agent Jefferson. The woman before her had an unyielding determination that flirted with obsession.

"What's her motive? Why kill all those men?" the coroner's voice held a mix of fear and curiosity.

"She's a ghost. No clear motive that we could find," Jefferson replied sharply. "But we suspect it was a criminal dispute. The whole thing smacks of a gangland-style massacre. She may be involved in illegal arms dealing, possibly trafficking. She's dangerous. If any of the locals find any trace of her, they should not engage alone," Jefferson warned sternly.

The coroner's tone shifted, becoming more cautious. "She sounds like a professional killer."

"You have no idea," Jefferson responded with chilling finality.

Anna closed her eyes in the darkness of the refrigerator compartment, letting the weight of Agent Jefferson's words sink in. "Keep an eye out," Jefferson continued. "She might still be in town. Hell, she might be watching us right now. She always seems to show up one step ahead."

The thought struck like a bullet, precise and shattering. Anna's left hand formed a fist, the other poised like a phantom trigger. Tracked. By Jefferson. In Clearwater. Fear, an unfamiliar guest, invited itself in.

"Clearwater is small," the coroner noted, oblivious to the intruder mere feet away. "A woman like that—she'd stand out... if she's here, I mean."

The chill of the fridge compartment seeped into Anna's bones. Muscles tensed, and her breaths came shallow and measured. Eyes adjusted to the pitch black, she could make out nothing. But she didn't need to see. She needed to listen. And wait.

The voices outside were now muffled by their movement as the pair turned for the exit. The coroner's words, a low rumble. Jefferson's replies, clipped and authoritative. A clink of metal on metal as the coroner settled some tools, and receding footsteps. Anna counted each one, syncing their retreat with her escalating hope. They were leaving. The office would be empty soon.

"Did you leave this open?"

Anna's body went rigid. Her breath catching as her body readied itself like the hair-trigger of a pistol, primed to fire her from the morgue drawer and into a fight. The handle, near her feet, seemed to grin back at her like a cold specter. She could almost feel its movement if the coroner chose to pull. In her mind, Anna traced the layout of the office, the exact steps to the exit, the weight of the door. Her fingers twitched, recalling the grip of her weapon, the trigger tension. She *couldn't* get locked in here.

Steps approached, each one a hammer strike against the tile in the silent exam room.

Dammit. He was coming directly toward her. Jefferson and the coroner... Shit.

A creak. A minor shift in pressure as the coroner paused before her compartment.

"Everything okay, doc?" Jefferson called out.

"I... yes, yes. I must've left this open."

She saw his shadow flicker as the coroner reached out and began to ease the door shut.

Anna's heart skipped a beat. Her fear and horror focusing to a moment of decision. If he locked her in here, with no way to escape, who knew when he'd return?

But if she emerged now?

Jefferson would try to arrest her—maybe—after all, Anna was a 'dangerous serial killer'. Either way, she'd have to fight her way out, close-quarters with a grieving FBI agent between her and the door. Guns would be drawn, tensions high. The battlefield math was instantaneous.

If Anna leapt out now, the odds were good one of them would end up shot.

Shit.

Her neck bristling, Anna raised her heel toward the door, ready to slam it back into the coroner's face—she prepared to make a break for it. Hard and fast.

But then, she went still, her fingers curling, just a little.

No. No, she couldn't let panic take over. No one had to die here.

Swallowing hard, her lungs shivering in her chest, Anna closed her fingers, pulling her ankle back from the hatch.

Click.

The last sliver of light slipped away. The latch engaged as the coroner gave the handle a little tug to ensure it had caught.

She was trapped.

Chapter 11

Hours... hours she'd tried to pry at the door. Hours in the cold... Anna could feel her body trembling now as she slowly lost precise control of her fingers to the shivering slowly overtaking her.

"Great... just great," she muttered. This was the closest Anna allowed herself to get to outright despair. In the field, an operative had to watch what they thought and what they said nearly as much as a soldier on the battlefield.

Too often, a soldier's mind could be their own worst enemy. And behind enemy lines, there was no one available to give a pep talk or whisper encouragement. If she didn't fan her own flame, the fire would go out. Simple as that.

"Just a bit more," she whispered again. "Just a bit..."

It had taken almost an hour just to maneuver herself around in the cramped space. Her elbow jamming into the ribs of the dead woman sharing the morgue cupboard, her hand pushing off the cold, metal compartment wall. Inch by inch, she'd slowly turned in the small space, grimacing occasionally as she did. More than once, she'd had to restart, as her spine compressed or her arm threatened to break.

At one point, she'd even considered snapping her arm just to make space. But in the end, she'd managed with just dislocating her right shoulder, and popping it back in once she'd finally managed to turn fully and face the door with both her hands in front of her, available to work on the hinges.

Still grimacing, she tried, for the hundredth time, to pry at the lock.

It simply wasn't working. She held her knife in one hand, pushing against the hinges now... But save a few superficial cuts on her knuckles from slippage, she hadn't so much as managed to budge a single hinge.

And now, desperation was beginning to set in.

"Shit," she whispered under her breath.

The chill of the cadaver refrigerator compartment had reached into Anna's marrow. She crouched in the cramped space, her breath a ghost against the stainless steel that entombed her. Her karambit knife, a talon of strong, full-tang steel, a familiar weight in her left hand, had been her salvation more times than she could count. But this was no enemy flesh; this was cold metal. Hinges. Stubborn and unyielding.

Anna prodded the hinge with the blade tip, seeking a weakness, any crevice to exploit. The compartment's design left no room for error, no convenient outcrop or ledge to leverage strength against. Her phone lay next to her, nearly drained of battery, the bright light shining.

For one brief moment, she'd considered calling Beth... But her soul had rebelled against the thought of putting her sister in danger.

No... No, this was her fault. She would figure a way out without dragging her baby sister further into it. Besides, with Jefferson sniffing around, likely aided by her FBI associates, things were getting more dangerous by the second.

Anna's fingers traced the smooth surface, frustration mounting with each passing second. The blade slipped, a screech of metal on metal, and Anna let out a hiss, the only small sign of her mounting frustration. Eyes darting in the dim light, she inventoried her meager options. The phone—too valuable a lifeline to risk damaging it. Besides, she needed torque. Something that fit between the gap of the hinges. Soft enough to fit due to malleability, but hard enough for leverage.

The thin lockpick set in her pocket was sturdy enough for setting pins not forcing a hinge or latch. Her phone would crack—and it wouldn't fit. The buckle on her belt? Too flimsy to withstand the force needed, and not malleable. Each option dismissed, each second counting. Her sniper-trained eyes missed nothing, yet offered no solutions.

"Think, damn it," she hissed under her breath, the words barely a whisper in the tomb-like silence. Her mind, trained for combat and survival, rifled through lessons learned in SEAL school, sniper tactics, demolition expertise. All reduced to naught in the face of a simple mechanical barrier.

She needed leverage. A fulcrum. Anna knew the principles of physics well, understood the need for a pivot point to amplify her force. Yet the sterile environment was devoid of loose objects, stripped of anything not bolted down or ensconced within the walls themselves.

Time ticked by, measured only by the rise and fall of her chest as she took slow, controlled breaths. Panic was a luxury she couldn't afford, an indulgence that had no place in her regimented world. Her past as a government assassin had drilled into her one truth—to survive, one must adapt.

And Anna Gabriel was a master of adaptation.

But that didn't change the facts. She needed something metallic but malleable. Firm, but small. Something to wedge behind the hinge, providing a fulcrum...

Anna's breath came in shallow bursts, her left hand clutching the curved knife like a lifeline. The cadaver, an involuntary companion in her icy prison, offered no assistance with its pallid silence. For the better part of her escape attempt, Anna had tried to ignore it, tried to pretend it wasn't there. But compartmentalization was difficult even in the best of circumstances.

The chemical smell of the body in the coroner's fridge was what got to her the most.

"Shit," she whispered, as an idea struck her.

She glanced slowly down at the corpse, wincing. An older body... Fillings? No... but sometimes... sometimes gold teeth?

Anna didn't often pray, but now, she offered up a small apology. "Sorry, God," was all she managed. If the Big Guy Upstairs was listening, she wasn't sure he'd be in a very understanding mood.

Still... A girl had to do what she had to do.

Reaching out with one finger, grimacing at the dirty work, and pushing aside the lips of the corpse, Anna searched with her phone flashlight for some glimmer of hope.

And there it was.

Glinting dully in the harsh light—a single gold tooth. Anna recoiled slightly but steeled herself, reminding her racing heart that this was just another mission, albeit an unconventional one.

She lifted her knife.

The thought revolted her. She'd dealt death in fifteen countries; she'd seen the insides of men spill onto foreign soils, but this—desecrating the dead for survival—it scraped at what little remained of her conscience. Still, necessity clawed at her resolve, and Anna knew hesitation could mean a permanent stay in this cold tomb.

"Sorry, friend," she muttered to the cadaver, the words feeling hollow and absurd in the context. Her left hand steadied the flashlight beam on the deceased's mouth, casting stark shadows across her features. With a practiced grip, she positioned the blade at the gumline of the gold tooth.

The knife was not designed for dental work. The task was gruesome, requiring force where finesse should have prevailed. The sound of metal against enamel echoed in the claustrophobic space, grating and unnatural. Anna worked with grim determination, ignoring the bile rising in her throat.

She pried. The tooth resisted. She leveraged her body against the wall, the chill of the metal seeping through her clothes—a reminder of the stakes. Seconds stretched into eternity until, with a final, determined twist, the gold tooth relinquished its hold.

It came free with a sickening pop, and Anna clutched it, the metal cold against her skin. It felt so small, and Anna had to focus not to lose the glittering nugget in her shivering fingers. But now she had her tools of escape: a gold tooth and a combat knife.

"Time to get to work," she whispered, steeling herself for the next phase of her escape.

With meticulous care, she wedged the gold tooth into the groove beside the hinge, the cold metal of the compartment biting into her skin as she leaned in for leverage. Her left hand, more dexterous, maneuvered the tooth into position while her right grasped the knife, the solid steel blade catching the light like a threat.

Her movements were deliberate, every shift of weight calculated. The makeshift fulcrum lodged firmly in place, and she pressed the edge of the knife against it. The metal groaned, a low protest in the silence of the morgue.

"Come on," Anna hissed, a whisper torn from her throat.

She applied pressure, her muscles tensing like coiled springs. The gold tooth held, an unlikely ally amidst the stainless steel and death. Tension mounted, the strain singing through her arms. A bead of sweat traced a cool line down her temple, ignored. Her focus narrowed to the hinge, the gold, the knife. She pushed harder, the effort etching lines of resolve deep into her features.

Suddenly the metal creaked, a mean, groaning sound like an old man being shaken awake against his will.

Patience. Pressure. Repeat.

The rhythm became a mantra, each moment stretching taut between success and entrapment.

Then, a shift—a minute give in the structure. Anna grit her teeth, a half-mad grin breaking out as she focused on the levered point of her knife. Then with a final, jarring screech, the first hinge gave way. It came free, and Anna lurched at the sudden shift in the hatch panel. A millimeter gap letting in fresh air like a whisper.

"Halfway," Anna breathed, no time for relief or celebration. Her mind had already moved to the next task, the next hinge.

Setting the gold tooth against the second hinge, her left hand steadied the knife as her right hand applied the force. She pushed, the knife's edge biting into the metal as a curl of misting breath rolled from between her lips. Her hand remembered the grip, the pressure, the angle—no room for error.

The second hinge resisted, stubbornly as if petulantly defying her silent command to yield. Anna's jaw clenched. The space was tight, her body contorted uncomfortably. Sweat mingled with the chill that clung to her skin. But discomfort meant little to a woman who had endured worse in far-flung corners of the world. In those places, she had learned one thing: survival wasn't about comfort. It was about will. And she had to survive. Beth was counting on her and —Sammie.

A low groan emanated from the metal. The sound was satisfaction, affirmation. Another push, her muscles tensed, and then it gave way. Hinge two, done. A small noise escaped her—a quick gasp of effort.

Anna paused, a millisecond to acknowledge the progress. The hinges were popped. Only the latch held the hatch to the morgue drawer closed. It would still require force to pop it open.

Leaning forward, Anna tried to brace her shoulder against the cramped panel back, her palms gripping for any kind of leverage around her. She shoved forward, once... twice. But despite the crunching bang that rippled through the steel, the door did not give way.

Closing her eyes for a moment, collecting herself, Anna began the slow process of turning herself back around, rotating in the tight space to put her heels back against the door again. It was easier the second time, and she didn't need to dislocate her shoulder to get back in position like she had before.

Placing her back against the compartment wall, feet braced against the door, Anna took one deep breath. Her focus sharp. Heartbeat steady. The kick would need to be strong, precise.

Her legs were coiled springs. Her boots, weapons. She aimed, the target clear in her mind. Kick. The impact reverberated through her bones. Breathe. Kick again. Metal bent, protested. Breathe. Kick. Over and over, rhythm relentless.

The lock bent. The hinges gone, only the small piece of metal securing the door remained.

The door buckled, a loud clang on impact. Anna's boots connected again, metal groaning under the assault. Once more, heel against steel. The door careened from its frame, clattering onto the cool linoleum outside the compartment with a final, resounding crash.

Anna unfurled from her crouched position, muscles protesting. She stepped over the threshold, eyes adjusting to the dim light of the coroner's office. Silence enveloped the room, thick and waiting. She stood still, listening, every sense sharpening.

The coroner's tools lay scattered on a stainless-steel table, reflecting the faint glow of overhead lights. Vials of chemicals sat untouched in their racks, labels facing outward. Cabinets loomed against the walls, their contents hidden behind closed doors.

Breath steady, Anna moved forward. She cataloged everything—the position of chairs, the layout of desks, the locations of exits. Her gaze swept the room, a silent sentinel. No movement save for the soft sway of her own shadow cast by the flickering fluorescent light above.

Eyes narrowed, she scanned for anomalies. A drawer was slightly ajar, its contents possibly disturbed. Papers lay strewn across the floor under a desk, edges curling.

No sound betrayed another presence. No scent carried the warning of recent activity. Still, she knew better than to let her guard down. She stepped lightly, avoiding the papers by her foot, making her way toward the exit. But then, she hesitated.

Her eyes slipped to the desk. Back to a small, plastic compartment on the gurney by the desk.

Anna's focus tightened. There, glinting under the harsh light—a small, metal object resting atop the gurney. It beckoned, an out-of-place beacon amongst white sheets and clinical tools. It was the microcapsule Agent Jefferson and the coroner had been discussing, the one pulled from the Mayor's arm during his autopsy.

The metal was nondescript, unassuming. But she knew better. She drew her phone from her pocket. She captured the item's image—its size, its form, its enigmatic purpose. Every angle documented. Light bounced off its surface, revealing minute engravings, subtle imperfections.

"Capture everything," she muttered, a mantra for precision.

This was what had killed the mayor. What had likely killed the man by the lake.

She'd never seen its like before.

Photos taken, Anna moved quickly. Time was currency, and she was spending it fast. She attached the images to a message, her thumb hovering, then pressed send. Casper would receive them within seconds. His insight was crucial. His analysis, imperative.

She dialed his number, phone pressed against her ear, the ringtone sounding like a countdown. A click, then his voice cut through the static of anticipation.

"Got something," she said, words clipped with urgency. "Photos sent. Need ID on the metal item."

"Nice to hear from you, too," came the terse reply.

"Fast, Casper. No time to waste."

"Copy that. Anything can you tell me about it?"

"Caused a pulmonary embolism," she said. "Possibly by releasing air into the blood stream. Coroner found it embedded in a dead man's arm."

"Oh, shit. Okay. We thinking professional wetwork? It doesn't exactly look homemade."

She pushed out into the hall, shaking her head. "I have no idea. But it's not something I've seen before. Maybe repurposed med-tech?"

The corridor was silent, the dim light casting long shadows against the bright, clean walls, and Anna moved with precision, her combat boots barely whispering against the linoleum. Each step was measured, deliberate. The window at the end of the passageway, her safest point of egress, loomed closer.

Casper grunted in affirmation, clearly inspecting the pictures on his end as he spoke. "Could be. I'll run it by my sources, see if anyone recognizes it."

Anna gave a clipped nod, quickly checking the corners as she made for an exit. "One other thing," she added, the phone still against her cheek.

"Can't this wait until morning?"

"Asshole, I just spent hours trapped in a cold box with a corpse."

"Wha...? Nevermind. I don't want to know. You do you."

Anna rolled her eyes, shaking out her hair and pushing her distinctive white streak behind her ear. She nearly shot back a joke of her own, but the words died as she remembered her encounter at the plant earlier that morning, and instead her voice cut low, hard and serious.

"Did you tell Landon Byers I was going to be in Maine?"

The moment she asked the question, the line went silent.

"Casper," she demanded when the former SEAL failed to answer.

"Anna, I—"

"Did you tell Byers?"

"Of course not," he protested. "But he was sniffing around is all. Just asking what I knew about some of the old guard. You know how he is."

"Sniffing because you left a trail?" She couldn't mask the accusation in her tone.

"Nah... just, following his own leads."

"Leads that point to me? We had an agreement. You didn't even know I was in Maine."

"I had a guess."

"Dammit."

"Yeah, well, Landon's good people. Anyhow, it was a couple weeks ago."

"Yeah, well, he's here too."

"What?"

"Took some job. Private security. There was a kid in a basement."

"That's not Landon's style. If he'd known about a kid, he'd never have signed up."

"You sure?"

"He's a good friend, Anna. I trust him."

"Yeah? The meeting didn't feel *friendly*."

"How unfriendly we talking?"

"Certain words were exchanged. And bullets."

Casper sighed into the phone receiver, and Anna could almost imagine the big man running his calloused fingers through that bristle brush beard of his as he chewed on the idea. "Were you doing anything... untoward?"

"Gotta define the big words for me, boss."

"Thought so. Look, I didn't know he was going to follow you to Maine."

"So, he did?"

"Sounds like it. When he called me a couple weeks ago, he was in Bali."

Anna cursed. "What the hell does he want?"

"You'd have to ask him."

"Can't. Busy with my own shit."

"Alright... Well, I have no idea what Byers is doing. But I can look into this metal Tic Tac you sent. Try and figure out what it is or where it came from. Anything else?"

"Stop talking to people about my business," Anna added, briskly.

As she reached the window at the end of the hall, her fingers traced the latch, flipping it with a muted click. She hoisted herself up, muscles coiled and tense. The window gave way silently, opening to the night's embrace as she slipped silently outside.

"I... Landon isn't people. He's one of us. One of the good ones. You know he saved my life in Beirut. Twice. Well, once and a half."

"I'm serious, Casper. Keep my name, my sister's name, my whole family out of your mouth."

"Alright. Shit. My bad. But for what it's worth, I think you should talk. He said he had something for you."

"Don't care."

There was a moment of dead air where Anna glanced at her phone to be sure the line hadn't dropped. As she did, she glanced back at the morgue window, now just a rectangle of faint light in a wall of midnight darkness behind her.

With a tired sigh, Casper shifted on the other end. "Fine. My lips are sealed. Sorry."

Anna gave a quick, jerking nod, slowly relaxing her grip on her phone. She hadn't realized how tightly her fingers had clamped down, but as she did, she could hear the cool plastic of the phone case creaking. "Keep it that way," she said. "Look into that item I sent. I need it pronto."

"Magic word?"

She snorted. "You've been spending too much time with Waldo."

Chapter 12

Anna didn't remember the last time she'd slept well into the first rays of morning light. But twice now, drifting in and out, she remained lying there as bright light shone through the blinds. Her bones still felt cold after last night's ordeal.

Beth was still asleep on the couch in the back of the RV. She hadn't woken when Anna had snuck in last night, and judging by how exhausted she'd looked, even lying there, she'd been through her own ordeal.

Every now and then, Anna could hear Sammie whimpering next door, where Beth had given him her bed. Nightmares, most likely.

The faint mewling sounds cut at Anna's heart. How was she supposed to convince Beth to leave town, now?

The boy didn't want to return to his mother, and he wouldn't tell them why. His father was dead. And they were stuck with him until Anna figured out what was going on. But on top of it all, Jefferson was breathing down their necks.

She kept her eyes closed, willing sleep to return. Once Casper got back to her... then she might have a lead. Until then... rest.

Even as this thought continued to cycle through her mind, the stillness shattered—three sharp raps against metal. Anna's eyes snapped open. Training took over. Heartbeat steady; breaths shallow.

The second round of banging was louder, urgent.

"Damn it," Anna muttered as she swung her legs off the bed, every muscle coiled tight. She reached under her pillow, fingers closing around the cool grip of her pistol—a habit from tours spent in places where waking up alive wasn't a given.

She padded across the cramped space, left hand leading. Her right hand, the one that could handle a firearm with equal precision if need be, gripped the weapon at her side. The digital clock on the counter read 10:17 AM.

Bare feet silent on the vinyl floor, Anna approached the door, her shadow merging with the dark outlines of her mobile sanctuary. Another series of knocks, impatient. She peered through the peephole, pistol ready.

She blinked, stunned.

Stared some more, then blinked again.

"What the hell..." she whispered under her breath.

Casper.

His figure loomed outside, imposing even through the distorted fish-eye lens. Tattoos crawled up his arms. His jaw was set hard, and his shades—for once appropriate in the sharp morning sun—veiled his eyes.

Anna's hand hesitated on the lock, senses straining. What brought Casper here? What did he want?

Decision made, she disengaged the lock with a click and pulled the door open. They stood face-to-face.

"Anna." His voice was gravel, low and strained.

"Talk," she said, her own voice a whisper-thin command.

Casper's fist clenched and unclenched, an erratic piston on the brink of malfunction. "Why, Anna? Why drag me into this mess?"

"Drag you into what?" she countered, her stance grounded like a tree's roots to the earth, pistol still unseen but ready.

"Stop playing games!" His voice was a pummeling force, a battering ram against her calm.

Her brow furrowed, not in fear, but puzzlement. She took a step back, space needed for clarity, or escape. "Explain."

He paced before her, a caged animal just shy of gnawing off its own limb. The silence stretched taut between them, a high wire neither could traverse without risk.

"Talk to me, Casper." Her words cut the air, sharp, precise.

His mouth opened, but no sound emerged. Tension coiled in his throat, visible through the tight skin of his neck.

Anna's mind raced as she considered the implications of Casper's presence.

How exactly had he found her?

He was good... but not even Casper was that good. Trackers. Had to be. She'd sweep the RV, scan every nook and cranny. No more surprises.

She heard Sammie whimper again from the backroom, Beth stirring as the noise broke the midmorning quiet.

"Outside," Anna said, her voice low, commanding despite the tremor of uncertainty that threaded through it. The morning air held a chill, a shiver creeping up her spine not entirely from the cold.

Casper stepped out first and Anna followed, shutting the door with a soft click behind her. Gravel crunched under their boots as they moved away from the RV, creating distance.

The lot was deserted. A sea of asphalt lay around them, empty but for her RV sitting solitary under the thin shadow of a sleeping lamppost. The space between them felt charged.

What the hell was he doing in Maine?

First Landon Byers... now Casper?

"Talk," Anna prompted, her eyes scanning the area, never settling.

Casper's jaw tightened, the muscle there jumping with tension. "You know why I'm here."

"Assumptions can kill," Anna replied, steady.

He turned, facing her with a scowl. "You did this... whatever hornet's nest you made me kick over."

"What?"

He turned his phone to her, showing the image of the small, metal pill she'd sent him last night.

She blinked. "So... you know what it is?"

Casper's chest heaved, a caged bull ready to charge. Dark shades hid his eyes, but they could not mask the fury etched into the clenched line of his jaw.

"Two men. Armed." His words hit with the force of bullets. "They came after I did an image search for this thing."

She blinked, "Excuse me?"

"You heard me. An hour after I started looking into this, they showed up at my door."

"How? I thought you encrypted your web searches."

"I do."

And now she could hear the strain in his voice. She could almost feel his eyes boring into hers, even hidden behind those ridiculous glasses of his. But the fear... now it made sense.

Someone had tracked him. And he didn't know how. Tracking others—it was his advantage. His job. But to be tracked himself... It was troubling him.

He was scared.

Anna's stance faltered for a fraction of a second. Her mind reeled.

"Armed? How?"

"Automatics. No hesitation in their step. They knew what they were looking for," Casper said, spitting out the facts like spent shell casings. "Me."

"Did they follow you here?" Her voice remained even.

"Can't be sure. But they got my place turned over pretty good before I gave them the slip." Casper's hands flexed, eager for a fight that had come and gone.

"Tell me again. Who were these guys? Two?"

"Two guys. Armed," Casper recounted. "Professional. No badges, no warrants, just guns and questions."

"And?"

"Let's say we negotiated." A brief lift of Casper's mouth hinted at a scuffle; the bruise on his knuckles confirmed it. "They were after what I'd found. Data. Names. Places. Your name."

Her training screamed danger, her instincts coiled ready. They were exposed here, two targets on an open range. "You give them anything?"

"Nothing." His assurance was granite, but his eyes held the faint spark of fear. "And that's when they tried to shoot me."

"How'd you get away?"

He snorted. "They might've tracked me, but they don't know all my damn tricks. I triggered the alarm smoke."

"Smoke alarm?"

"No. The alarm smoke. When the alarm goes off, my house fills with smoke. They tried to shoot me anyhow. Busted up my favorite photo of the Dodge Camaro I used to own."

His voice sounded forlorn now as it so often did when one of his vehicles got so much as a scratch. Some people were gearheads or car enthusiasts. Casper was obsessed.

"So," he said, more firmly, holding up his phone, showing her the image of the metal device. "What the hell have you gotten me into?"

"I don't know," Anna said quietly. She glanced across the parking lot, a faint shiver flaring up her spine. "So you flew directly to me?" she asked, raising an eyebrow.

"Landon had a guy."

She stared at him. "Landon again..."

"It was scheduled for next week. But I expedited. His guy was luckily still at the airfield."

Casper was shifting from one foot to the other, arms crossed, eyebrows furrowed.

"Hang on," Anna said, cautiously. "You were going to come to Maine to meet Landon?"

"A week from now."

"Why a week?"

"He said it might take a week to convince you."

"Convince me of what?"

Casper just shrugged. "Ask Landon."

"I'm asking you."

"I don't know... he wanted to meet both of us. Told me he had a proposition." Casper shrugged.

"I don't want what he's selling."

"I'm telling you, Anna, he's one of the good ones."

"I don't even know what the hell that means." Anna paused. She could hear Beth calling Sammie's name from the RV.

She took a few more steps away from her mobile home, and lowering her voice, she whispered, "Look, I don't know what Landon is up to... or what you know, but I want no part of it. Once I finish up in this place, I'm gone. And you better believe this time I'm not telling you where."

He grimaced. "I'm not happy either, Anna. They burnt my damn home down."

"You rented."

"Still. I had stuff."

"Yeah, like what?"

"Computers. Servers. Guns," he added. "Thank God they didn't get Cammy. Had to leave her parked at the airport."

She rolled her eyes at the mention of his purple Charger.

"So what the hell is it?" she asked, pointing at the image on his phone.

"Proprietary technology," he said. "Made by a company in Silicon Valley."

"What's it doing in the arm of a mayor in Maine?"

He shook his head. "Don't know."

"What sort of proprietary tech?"

He shook his head. "It took some digging to find this, mind you. Found a prototype released ten years ago at a tech conference. Five years later, all mention of it vanished."

"Means someone bought it and wanted it hushed."

"Probably."

"So this tech company..."

"Not a tech company."

"What sort, then?"

"Military," he said simply. "Arms manufacturing."

She stared at him. "Called what?"

"LMX Corp," he said.

"Shit. Second largest in the US, right?"

"Aiming to be first largest," he replied. "It's a multi, multi billion dollar industry."

Anna's mind was racing as she tried to make sense of the information. Military technology, an anonymous buyer, and a mysterious company with a lot of money at stake. What the hell had she gotten herself into? But one thing was certain: she needed to keep her distance from Landon and his associates.

She glanced at Casper, whose gaze was unwavering. "So, it's a weapon or a device of some sort?"

Casper shook his head. "I'm not sure. Our contact in the military intelligence department said it's some sort of surveillance gear. But the way it was hidden in that mayor's arm... it's not a device that was meant to be found. I'm guessing it was surveillance with a built in fail-safe."

"So they implanted it... used it to control him. Then killed him? Why?"

He shrugged. "Dunno."

"But why a mayor in Maine?" she said. "It makes no sense."

Anna's heart pounded in her chest. She knew all too well about surveillance gear and how dangerous it could be. If someone was using it to control figures in government, it could lead to serious consequences.

"Answer that question," Casper said simply, "And you'll start unraveling all of this, I bet."

Anna considered this a second longer. "So those men... the ones who came for you. They showed up within an hour?"

"Yeah."

"Tracking you?"

"Somehow. Don't know. Something beyond what I know of, that's for sure."

"So some kind of high-level military tech."

"Possibly. Why? What are you thinking?"

"I'm thinking..." Anna murmured quietly. "That we see if those same guys are worried about image searches in Clearwater, too."

"Shit. Anna, no. No, this is a bad idea."

But she was already shaking her head. "Let's see if we can lure them here. I want some answers. If a couple of thugs with automatic weapons show up... I can't think of anyone who'd I'd rather chat with."

Casper let out a long sigh of frustration, but he didn't protest. He knew her well enough not to try and dissuade her once her mind was made up.

"And I need your help," she added.

"Does it pay?"

"I can give you some words of affirmation."

"Afraid my price is a bit higher than that, this time, Guardian."

"Yeah well, how about we call it even for ratting me out to Landon."

"By my count, you owe me for my house."

"That wasn't my fault."

"Yeah, well—perspective."

"Dammit, Casper..."

"Look, here's the deal." Casper fixed her with a stare, tilting his sunglasses to make eye contact. "I help you trap these assholes... they owe me a new shotgun. And in return, you take a meeting with Landon. Hear him out."

Anna frowned.

"Just hear him," Casper emphasized. "No promises or anything. Just listening. That's all I ask."

She bit her lower lip, considering it. "I'm telling you now, Casper, I want nothing to do with him or what he's involved in."

"That's fair," he said. "But just let him say what he's here to say, okay? Indulge me this once?"

Anna sighed heavily. "Fine. But if this turns out to be another mess..."

"It won't," he promised. "I'll make sure of it."

With an apprehensive nod, she agreed to his terms. Despite her reservations, she understood the gravity of the situation they were entangled in. The mention of LMX Corp and their clandestine operations had put her on edge, but the need for answers propelled her forward, even if it meant entertaining the notion of a meeting with Landon.

"So first things first," she said. "How exactly did you draw the termites out of the woodwork?"

"You want them here?"

"No... but nearby. I have a spot in mind."

Chapter 13

Anna melded with the underbrush, her homemade ghillie suit a patchwork of the forest floor. Crisp leaves and matted earth clung to her as she lay still, breaths measured and silent. The sniper rifle, an extension of her left arm, was poised against her shoulder. Her eye pressed to the scope, steady, scanning.

The small motel squatted at the edge of the lake, its timeworn walls bleached by weather. Double-story, L-shaped—each room fronted by glass, curtains drawn tight against prying eyes. A neon sign flickered in the mid-day sun half-heartedly: "No Vacancy" it lied; Anna knew better. Behind the structure, the parking lot lay empty, with only the haphazard flickering of shadows from the birds scavenging loose seeds and bugs from cracks in the asphalt.

The same motel they'd been in only the night before.

She shivered under the noon sunlight where she lay in the copse not twenty feet from the faint, lingering scent of ash where the body of the hitman had been discarded.

The lake, a silent witness, lapped gently at the shore, mirroring the anxious wait. Five hundred yards away, the parking lot's cracked asphalt sprawled out like a welcome mat for trouble. Each line marking the spaces was faded, the boundaries blurred—much like the moral lines Anna now faced. This was familiar territory for her: a battleground without the formality of war.

A breeze whispered through the trees, rustling leaves, brushing against Anna's cheek. She didn't flinch. Every sense sharpened for the impending arrival—the crunch of gravel, the low hum of an engine, the soft click of a safety being released.

Anna shifted minutely, the rifle's butt snug against her well-worn tactical vest. The weapon was sighted in. No room for error. Not now.

"Check your six, Casper," Anna's voice was a low growl in the stillness, barely disturbing the airwaves. "Eyes up. It's about to get busy."

Across the lake, hidden by the distance and his own camouflage, Casper responded with a static crackle. "Copy that, Anna. I'm set. Support is a go."

The radio went silent. A pact of mutual reliance stretched thin across the water, strong as steel wire.

Anna adjusted her position slightly, muscles tense beneath the makeshift ghillie suit. Grass and leaves clung to the fabric, making her one with the underbrush.

Then, movement.

An engine growled from the bend around the lake, the first hint of action. A black SUV rolled into the lot, gravel crunching like bones under its weight. Its approach was slow, predatory.

She counted the doors slamming—one, two, three...six in total. Six men emerged, their silhouettes etched by the motel's flickering neon sign. In a mix of casual clothing and baseball caps, the men looked like they could have been a group of drinking buddies out late after a football game. If not for the purposeful strides, athletic builds, and the way they held their weapons with professional competence, Anna might have even thought they had the wrong group.

"Not two this time," Casper's voice whispered in her ear.

I can count, she thought.

"Targets on site," Anna whispered into the radio, her thumb pressed against the transmit button.

"Copy. Let them play their hand first," Casper's voice held steady, a counterpoint to the adrenaline surging through Anna's veins.

The armed men moved toward the small utility shed behind the motel—the shed where Casper had rigged the internet router, connecting to the AI imaging software which had broadcast the picture she'd taken in the coroner's lab across all ISPs.

Boots thudded on the asphalt, hands gripping rifles and pistols. They communicated in terse nods and sharp gestures, a language of violence that Anna knew all too well. Out front of the pack of men walked a figure with the high-chinned profile of a natural-born leader, etched with sharp angles—a chiseled jawline, a hawkish nose, and eyes that glittered with a cold, calculating intelligence. His every movement exuded confidence, a dangerous allure that spoke quietly of his capacity for violence. Anna's gaze remained locked on him, unwavering and focused, her own features shrouded by the camouflage of her ghillie suit.

As she exhaled, slow and controlled, her rifle's crosshairs danced over the leader. Despite his predatory eyes darting about and the escort of gunmen, he was oblivious to the Guardian Angel. For now.

He approached the shed with two men carrying automatics at his side, the other three remaining by the SUV they rode in on.

She would wait until they found the radio they'd hidden in the shed. Until they were far enough from their vehicle that going back would prove too costly to consider. And sure enough, it didn't take long before the men reached the decoy shed. Anna could see their hushed conversations through the scope of her rifle. The leader barked out orders, his voice carrying authority and menace in equal measure. She could almost feel the tension radiating off him, a palpable energy that prickled her skin even from a distance.

Casper's voice crackled over the radio, breaking through the stillness of the moment. "On target."

She acknowledged Casper's words with a slight tilt of her head, her grip on the rifle steady as she watched the scene unfold before her eyes. The men rummaged inside the shed, their movements hurried yet purposeful. It wouldn't be long now before they discovered the hidden transmitter that had led them there.

A bead of sweat trickled down Anna's temple, her heartbeat thrumming in her ears like a war drum. She knew that once they found the device, chaos would ensue. It was only a matter of moments before the delicate balance of power shifted in an explosive crescendo.

The leader straightened suddenly, a look of realization crossing his face. He turned sharply towards the Mercedes parked nearby, suspicion evident in his gaze.

He was holding the radio receiver.

"Bingo," Anna whispered.

A crack split the noon air, a sound almost lost in the expanse between her and the parking lot. The Mercedes' logo—a three-pointed star—vanished in a spray of metal and paint.

The men responded to the gunshot with shouts. Ducking where they stood, attempting to shelter by the shed.

"Stay where you are," Anna's voice cut through the radio, no louder than necessary. "Next shot will be your heads."

Judging by the sudden reactions, they could hear her loud and clear over the radio.

Men froze, their confusion tangible even from her distance. Scrambling for cover, they ducked behind the shed, the SUV, eyes wild, searching.

"Working on facial recognition IDs," Casper murmured, more to himself than to Anna.

The wind whispered through the underbrush, its passage a ghostly caress against Anna's ghillie suit. She perched motionless, green eyes focused through the scope, tracking the men huddled behind the black SUV.

"Who the hell is this?" snapped the leader's voice, replying over the radio.

She spotted his military cut bobbing around as he glanced one way, then the other, desperately searching for the source of the gunshot.

Anna didn't reply. She had the information now. She held the cards.

Casper was busy identifying the men based on long range photos. Now, she just had to keep them still.

It was in this moment, as the plan materialized, that Anna should've known a wrench would've been thrown.

Her phone glowed. A vibrating sound. The only number she hadn't blocked for this mission.

She stared.

Beth.

Licking her lips and taking a quick, sharp inhalation against her unease, Anna glanced through the scope once more. The men still hunkered down, looking around.

If Beth was calling, now, knowing at least vaguely what Anna and Casper were up to, it had to be bad. With a reluctant sigh, Anna tapped the answer button on her phone. "What's wrong, Beth?" Her voice was strained, the tension of the situation bleeding through even in this brief moment of distraction.

A static hiss preceded Beth's voice, jarring in the silence. "Anna. It's Sammie. He's gone. He took your gun."

Anna's heart rate spiked, and her breath caught, the shock quickly stifled by long-established discipline as her mind darted for the next piece of relevant information to solve the problem suddenly thrust upon her.

"Location?"

"I don't know. He just... vanished." The pitch of Beth's voice climbed, tight with fear.

"Lock down. Do *not* go out looking for him. I'll handle it." The words were clipped, a promise.

"Where are you?"

"Nearby. Taking care of that *errand*. I'll be back soon."

"Anna... I'm worried he's going to do something... Worried he'll get hurt. Why would he take the gun?"

"He's only ten, Beth."

"That's what I'm worried about."

Given the little they knew about Sammie and the danger he had faced after his father's death, Anna could at least guess at the spirit of what the pre-teen boy with the cut-up feet might be planning, but she didn't want to worry Beth needlessly. Speculation didn't help. Finishing the objective and getting onto tracking Sammie would.

"Gotta run, sis," Anna said. "Remember, *stay put.*"

Beth swallowed and gave a faint, shuddering sob. "Be careful."

"Always am."

Call ended.

Anna returned her focus to the parking lot. Across the expanse of water, well out of range or potential danger, Casper remained oblivious to the new crisis. His attention was on his screen, on the men crouched like cornered animals as he ran his facial recognition software.

Abruptly one of the men by the SUV shouted. Anna swiveled her sights, following the gunman's line of sight. He was peering across the lake in Casper's direction.

"Shit," Anna whispered.

In his hideaway, Casper had smeared the exposed plastic of his laptop with mud, cutting any ambient glare or reflections. But somehow a small flicker of reflection, no sharper than the sun glinting off a pair of glasses, was intermittently flashing from the hiding spot.

Gunfire erupted. Staccato bursts. Anna watched in horror across the lake as a tumble of jerky movements rose from his hiding spot among the trees while bullets peppered his position. Sparks danced on rocks. Splinters flew from trees. He was pinned, a target in a shooting gallery.

"Taking fire," Casper grunted into the radio.

"Cover," Anna replied. Brevity was key.

Her finger tensed near the trigger, ready. Eyes scanned. Calculations made. Wind direction noted. Breath held. Hands steady. All in under a second.

Casper's silhouette edged along his makeshift cover, seeking respite from the hailstorm of lead. Rounds chewed up the earth around him, a deadly rain.

"Suppressing," Anna announced.

Her rifle barked once. Twice. Precision over panic. Always control. The threat needed quelling, but the urgency to find Sammie clawed at her insides.

The rifle shots punched holes in the roof of the black SUV like the sound of a hammer striking an anvil. Non-lethal for now. She could've killed all six gunmen if she'd wanted. But she still didn't know what they were all involved in, and dead men wouldn't answer her questions.

But now they were shooting at her friend. And they hadn't taken the message.

Instead of hunkering down again, they continued shooting at Casper, emboldened by her missed shots and hustling into the wood that ringed the lake, cutting their way toward her pinned teammate.

Anna growled in frustration. "Returning fire," she snapped into the radio.

Motionless, her breathing shallow. Anna's eyes narrowed behind the scope. The crosshairs settled on the first target as he stepped into view.

"Red hat. Front."

Two heartbeats. A pull of the trigger. The man in the red hat staggered back, a silent collapse onto the gravel. No one had time to react.

"Next. Blue jacket. Left flank."

Another squeeze. Another body thudded against the unforgiving ground. The remaining men spun, confusion etched on their faces, weapons scanning for a phantom.

"Green shirt. Non-lethal." Her voice, a whisper to herself. The shot rang out. Green shirt crumpled, clutching his thigh, howling. Alive.

The air thickened with tension. Breath held. Each second, a step closer to resolution or disaster.

"Anna," Casper's voice was a thread of sound in her ear, "watch it!"

The fourth man, a lean fellow whose eyes were shadowed by a black beanie, turned toward Anna's sniper nest. He raised his rifle, aiming straight at her hidden form and time slowed. Anna's left hand steadied the rifle. Her right eye squinted. A fraction of movement as black beanie's muzzle flashed.

Anna's shot pierced the stillness—a sharper, deadlier retort. Black beanie dropped, gun skittering away on the asphalt. Silence returned, punctuated by groans and the distant lapping of lake waves.

"Four down," she breathed into the radio. "Sitrep?"

"Clear on my end. They're confused, scared."

"Good." Anna's gaze remained locked on the scene. "Stay ready."

She exhaled, the sound barely audible. Focus. Sammie needed her. But first, control. Always control.

She surveyed the fallen soldiers. Some groaning. The two remaining men motionless by the front bumper.

"Contain them," she said.

"Got it."

Anna broke into a sprint, racing through the leaves, her sniper rifle swung over her shoulder on its leather strap as she stripped the excess bulk of her ghillie suit in favor of more vision and mobility.

In under a minute, she reached the outskirts of the parking lot, her senses heightened, every muscle primed for action. The acrid scent of gun smoke lingered in the cool air, mixing with the earthy aroma of the forest. Her gaze swept over the chaotic scene before her, the fallen figures scattered like discarded puppets.

A figure was trying to sneak around the front of the car as she erupted less than three paces from him, the hawk-nosed leader of the small attack force. Anna aimed her handgun at his head, and he stared at her, wide-eyed, horrified, slowly rising to his feet.

"Hands," she commanded, her voice steel. The leader raised his hands, eyes locked on the barrel of Anna's handgun. Her finger hovered over the trigger; disciplined, poised.

"Kneel," she instructed. He complied, the gravel digging into his skin. His breaths came out in ragged gasps, punctuating the night with the sound of fear, his eyes glancing around but giving nothing away.

A rustle. A whisper of movement. Too close. Anna's neck bristled as electric instinct fired through her overwrought nerves.

Someone behind her.

She began to move, but too late.

"Don't you move!" snapped the voice.

Anna tensed. It was the sixth man. Silent steps. A gun barrel cold against her neck, she could almost feel him pulling the trigger. Her hand hovered above the paracord grip of her karambit, her instincts screaming for her to snatch up the steel talon and take her chances.

Instead, a shot echoed across the lake—Casper's shot.

Anna spun, her hooked combat knife coming up as she ducked inside the gunman's guard, knocking his pistol to the side. He didn't fight back, and Anna quickly stopped, inches from the look of stunned surprise etched on his face as he crumpled to the ground—a fresh bullet wound in his throat.

"Clear," Casper's voice crackled through the radio, calm amidst the turmoil.

Anna glanced across the expanse of water, knowing Casper was out there, watching over her with a hawk's vigilance.

"Thanks," Anna whispered into the radio, a nod to the unseen guardian across the lake. Her breath steadied as she turned back to the immediate threat—the leader of this assault team.

He was going for a sidearm, his eyes locked on Anna as he threw himself toward the SUV, trying to simultaneously take cover from Casper's shots across the small lake.

Anna lunged for him, her heart hammering as she darted like a snake to grasp the leader's gun arm by the wrist.

A twist, a yank.

The assault team leader's eyes widened in pain, and his pistol fell to the gravel with a harsh thud. Pivoting, Anna slammed her right elbow into his throat, cutting off his air, and the sharp-eyed leader sagged, his nerveless limbs dropping like a kite from a windless sky, unconscious before he hit the ground.

Anna's fingers were quick, securing the leader's arms behind him with zip ties from her pocket. Time was evaporating; every second counted. She hauled the limp body over her shoulder, an echo of countless drills, muscle memory guiding her through the motions. Sweat beaded on her forehead, mingling with the grime of battle.

That's one captive. Alive and in good enough condition to talk.

With swift, deliberate steps, Anna dragged the guard to Casper's rental vehicle, popping the trunk and letting him collapse into the dark nook, slamming it shut over him with a final muted *whump.*

Tapping the radio, Anna called out brusquely, "Casper, get your ass back here. We're moving out, double-time."

Six men. Five down. One captured. Area secured. And that meant—

"Sammie."

Chapter 14

"Pull over here," Anna said.

Casper nodded, swerving into the forest preserve entrance under the afternoon sun.

Gravel crunched underfoot as Anna yanked the assault team leader from the trunk of the rental car. His breath came in short gasps, a mix of fear and exertion as she propelled him toward the riverbank. The cold metal of her gun pressed against his skull; his knees hit the ground hard.

"John Martin," she said, her voice low and steady. "I know who you are."

The information came courtesy of Casper's facial recognition software—along with a few other juicy bits that had come up on the follow-up searches—meaning they were now armed with more than just a gun.

And yet, time was ticking, Sammie was still out there, and they were no closer to figuring out who was involved in all of this or where the son of the dead mayor had gone. But Anna suspected those two questions were not too distant from each other.

Anna could feel her promise to Beth eating at her conscience. She needed to get out there, to find the missing ten-year-old whose name had started this entire chain of violence.

But first things first.

The river flowed lazily beside them, oblivious to the tension that hung heavy in the damp air. John's hands were clammy, dirt smearing on his palms as he braced himself against the earth.

"LDX Corp," Anna continued, her grip on the gun unyielding. "That's your employer, isn't it?"

Her left hand adjusted its hold on the weapon, but she didn't flinch. Not a muscle trembled.

"Don't know what you're talking about," John began, his voice a broken whisper.

"Shut up." Her command cut through. The safety clicked off with a sound that echoed the finality of her intent.

The wind kicked up, covering the natural sounds so that even the river seemed to pause, waiting for what would come next.

Anna stood rigid, the gun unwavering in her grip. John Martin's breaths punctuated the silence, each one shallow and ragged. Casper, a few paces away, leaned against the trunk of a gnarled oak. He whistled a tuneless melody, scrolling through his phone with a detached air. The screen's glow danced on his impassive f ace.

"Did you know Maine's got beryl?" Casper's voice cut through the stillness, casual as if discussing weather. "Big deposits. And our dear mayor, God rest his soul, he wasn't keen on mining."

Anna's eyes flickered toward Casper, then back to John. Her finger tightened around the trigger. "A plant," she said, her words dropping like stones into the quiet. "That's what he was. Wasn't he, John?"

John's mouth opened, but only a dry click of his tongue against his teeth came out. Silence returned, thickening around them.

"His death," she continued, every syllable measured and heavy. "You had a hand in it. Didn't you?"

The gun remained steady. She'd learned long ago how to hold stillness, how to wait. How to make others squirm.

John's gaze flitted between the barrel of the gun and the dark water of the river. His knees dug into the wet earth, his breath misting in the cool air. Anna stood over him, the gun unwavering in her grip. The click of the safety echoed, a stark sound against the hushed rustle of the river.

"Talk," she said, the command stripped to its bones.

He shook his head, lips pressed into a thin line, eyes darting away from hers. She could see the calculation there, the desperate arithmetic of survival.

"Wrong answer." Her voice was flat, a blade laid bare.

Anna's thumb rested on the hammer of the gun, ready to cock it back. She watched him, watched the sweat bead at his temple despite the chill. She knew fear. She'd seen it in countless eyes. John's were no different.

"The chip in the mayor's arm," she began, her words paced to the rhythm of the flowing river. "You know about it."

His jaw clenched. A muscle twitched.

"That hitman, 'Jim Monroe'." The fake name of the man Beth and Anna had burned in the woods only a couple nights before hung between them. "Was he also one of yours?"

John was glancing side to side as if desperately searching for help that would never come.

"Speak, or the next thing you feel will be a bullet," Anna pressed, her finger ready to squeeze the trigger.

"I didn't have anything to do with any of it," he said, his voice hoarse.

"Bullshit," she snapped, her voice accusing.

"Casper," she called out, "Tell me more about Beryl-mining in Maine, why dontcha?"

She'd already scanned through the information on the drive over after Casper had shown it to her. LDX was tied to buying up beryl mines, and Maine was a holdout. It just so happened, the mayor—now dead—had built a platform on environmental concerns, shutting down the beryl mining.

For a company trying to build a monopoly on beryl, this was only good news.

So why was the mayor dead?

"Well," Casper called back. "Looks like beryl is used in fiber optic cables, electronics – all the stuff that makes the world go round. Clearwater's mayor seemed to think it was a good thing to shut down all that mining. Messed with some people's business plans, I'd wager."

Anna's gaze didn't waver from John Martin; his eyes darted between her and Casper, a flicker of realization dancing in his gaze.

"Why?" Anna demanded, her voice like steel. "Who killed him?" she asked with a warning edge.

John bit his lip, a bead of sweat trickling down the side of his face.

She kicked him backwards, and his head snapped back as his shoulders hit the muddy riverbank. His skull splashed into the water, and liquid dripped down the side of his face. Staring at her wide-eyed, John Martin fixated on the gun pointed at his skull.

"Last chance."

She fired two shots into the mud, sending up plumes of dirt and water.

John flinched, then glared at her through the water.

"Harrington," he muttered, his voice barely audible.

She nodded, her eyes narrowing.

"Harrington?" she repeated, her voice low and dangerous.

"Yes," John answered, his voice trembling, "Alfred Harrington is buying stock in the company. He's trying to shut down the mines. It was his idea. All his idea."

His words hung in the air like a curse.

Anna frowned, her grip tightening on the gun. Harrington... the same man who Sammie had reacted to on the television. The Harringtons were the wealthiest family in Clearwater, and one with mining connections. It made sense if he was buying into LDX Corp. And a monopoly on beryl mining would go a long way in helping an arms company.

Anna's grip on the gun was unwavering, her left hand steady as if cast from iron. The river lapped at the banks, a quiet observer to the unfolding drama.

"So... a weapons company buys a mayor. Lines his pockets. But five years ago, they line him with something else, right? The hitman too? You also? Are all of LDX's pawns chipped? Hmm? Did they tell you it could kill you, or is that just a fun little surprise?"

John's breathing hitched as Anna stepped back, gun still trained on his trembling form. The river flowed quietly beside them. Her eyes narrowed; they were a predator's eyes—locked on prey.

"John," she said, her voice low and steady, "you've got more than fear coursing through your veins."

He swallowed hard, the sound audible in the heavy silence, her words beginning to chip away at his resolve. She could see the slump of his limbs, the steady decline from thoughts of escape to thoughts of mere survival.

"LDX loves their toys," Anna continued, "like that little insurance policy embedded in your arm."

His gaze flickered down to his left sleeve, then back up, his Adam's apple bobbing with dread.

"Standard issue for your kind of work," Anna stated, matter-of-factly.

She reached to her thigh sheath and drew out her wicked, crescent-shaped karambit knife with its gleaming blade. It spun once in her hand before she leaned forward and cut the zip-ties from the man's wrist. "Do what you want. But Harrington's gonna find out you chatted. Come near us, and I'll bury you. You have my word."

She turned away, stalking back towards her partner-in-crime.

Casper stood a few paces behind, his face unreadable. But when Anna turned and caught his eye, the concern was there, stark against his usually impassive features. He lowered his sunglasses as she drew near, and neither of them looked towards the trembling form of their captive.

The big man's gaze shifted behind his dark sunglasses, a tic in his jaw the only sign of disquiet. "There's more," he said, voice low. "It's Landon... he's working with Harrington."

Anna's eyes narrowed, her breath slow and measured. The revelation hung heavy in the damp air.

"I thought you said he was one of the good ones."

"He is. He doesn't know. I'd bet anything. He could help us."

"Or he could kill us both."

"No. He won't. He took a cushy security gig to save some money for his next idea."

"Yeah? The idea he wants to speak to us about?"

"Speak to you, specifically," Casper said.

He led the way slowly back to the waiting car, and when Anna glanced back, John was stumbling along the river, away from them. She wasn't sure if letting him go was the right call, but Casper's words lingered in her mind. She straightened her back and followed him to the car.

As they got back into the vehicle, she couldn't shake the feeling that they were walking into a trap. The air was thick with uncertainty and danger. She glanced at Casper, his eyes meeting hers in the rearview mirror.

"You think we can trust him? Landon?" she asked, her voice tense.

Casper nodded, his expression grave. "We have to. We're running out of options."

She sighed, resting her head against the cool glass of the window. The forest blurred past them, a stark contrast to the danger that lurked within it. She knew she couldn't afford to trust easily. Her life had been damaged by trusting the wrong people, and the cost had been too high. Still, she couldn't deny that Casper's instincts were sharp.

"Harrington's gonna have a lot of security," Casper said, scratching through the thick beard covering his chin before wiping the sweat from the top of his bald head. "If he's able to afford Landon's fees... he's bankrolling a private army."

"And you think Landon will turn it down when we tell him where that money is coming from?"

"Landon plays the game for the pay. But he's not a criminal."

Anna shrugged, nodding once. "Let's test that theory. Besides... if I had to guess where Sammie was heading, it'd be the same spot. Harrington's."

"Sammie?"

"Yeah. Kid has a gun."

"Wait... what kid?"

"Just drive, I'll fill you in on the way."

Chapter 15

Anna and Casper crouched on the hill overlooking Harrington's massive, gated estate.

Below, the sprawling mansion was floodlit, casting eerie shadows on the neatly manicured lawns. The sharp lines of the building seemed to shout power and wealth. Anna's eyes scanned the property, searching for any signs of movement. The temperature had fallen, and a chill breeze blew across the hilltop, carrying with it the faint scent of pine. Evening had fallen, and night was approaching.

"There," she said, pointing to a far corner of the estate. "Looks like there's a pool house there. I think I saw movement."

Casper raised his binoculars, his fingers steady despite the wind. He focused on the small wooden structure nestled amongst the trees.

"There's a light on," he said, his voice low. "And I see movement inside."

Anna's heart rate quickened. Her training kicked in, and she began to plan their approach.

"We'll circle around the perimeter, staying as low as possible," she whispered. "Keep your eyes on the ground, and don't make a sound."

Casper nodded, his face set in determination. "We waiting until nightfall? That's a lot of guards down there."

"Private army," she replied. "I've spotted twenty at least."

"Sign of Landon?"

"None. He still not replying to your calls?"

"No."

"One of the good guys, huh?" she said, sarcasm dripping in her voice.

"He is. Maybe he found out what's up and dipped."

"Yeah. Likely."

Anna shifted in her crouched position on the grassy knoll, peering towards the estate below. It would take an hour or so more before the moon came out completely, and the darkness fell, but she wasn't sure they had that much time. There was no guarantee that Sammie was the one she'd spotted at the pool house, either.

Time was ticking.

Anna hadn't been back to the RV. She'd told her sister to hunker down and wait, and no doubt Beth would be worried—and when worried, there was no telling what her baby sister might do.

Anna let out a slow, deep exhale. Nightfall. They just needed to wait for more darkness so they could sneak in. They just needed to stick to the plan.

And then, all hell broke loose.

Shouting erupted, and Anna quickly locked onto a group of the guards by the fence pointing, their guns raised.

"Shit. It's him," Casper hissed.

The small form of a child had appeared by the pool house, his silhouette illuminated by the bright lights of an incoming Jeep.

Anna had already noted how everyone was on edge. Scared and tense. And now, at the arrival of a stranger the shouts went up, the barrels as well.

"God dammit, he's just a kid," Casper cursed, anger in his voice. But he kept his voice low.

"Hang on!" shouted a voice. But some of the men in the Jeep were either nervous or generally twitchy.

They opened fire, shooting in the direction of the small shadow by the pool house.

"Shit. Forget the plan," Anna snapped. "We're going in."

She flung herself towards the rental SUV, surging into the driver's seat. No time to go around.

They'd have to go straight through. Her eyes fixated on the fence at the base of the hill.

Casper was cursing, drawing his own gun as he arrived in the passenger side.

"Hang on!" she shouted.

Gunfire continued, scattering the night's silence. Shouts echoed. Anna floored the gas, and the engine screamed, pelting them towards the fence.

Some of the guards by the fence wheeled around, spotting them.

Still no sign of Landon Byers.

No sign of Alfred Harrington.

Bullets strafed the air around them, now split between the pool house and the rental SUV. The vehicle shook under the barrage, but she kept her eyes on the flicker of movement by the fence.

Casper swore, bracing himself against the dashboard as they plunged forward. The sound of the gunfire grew louder, punctuated by the occasional crack of bullets hitting the metal.

"You blow a tire and we're sitting ducks!" he called out.

Anna's teeth clenched, her white-streaked hair whipping as the vehicle bucked across the uneven ground. "No problem, just politely ask them to stop shooting."

The SUV lurched as they hit the fence, the monstrous vehicle crumpling the wrought iron gate under its immense weight. The fence tore apart under their relentless momentum, bending under the unnatural force of their onslaught. The windshield shattered with a loud crack as bullets hailed their progress, but Anna didn't falter. She drove straight into Harrington's estate, the engine roaring as they plowed through the property, leaving a trail of shattered fences in their wake.

The gunfire continued as they veered left, barreling down the road that led to the pool house. Casper fired out the window, returning fire with precision. Anna glimpsed a stray shot hit someone, but she couldn't afford to lose focus.

She swung the car around, slammed on the brake, and lurched out of the vehicle all in one motion.

"Take cover!"

"On it!"

Anna was already moving. More shouts erupted. She'd counted twenty men... but now more were appearing from inside the house. This guy... Alfred was taking his newfound stake in LDX Corp very seriously.

He had his own little military on his property. Whatever had gone wrong with the mayor, whatever had gotten the man killed... it all led back to Harrington.

But where was he?

And where the hell was Sammie?

In the chaos of the charge, she'd lost track of the boy. Thankfully, it looked like she wasn't the only one. Every guard in sight was aimed their way, taking cover as they closed in fast.

Anna cast around for their next move, and for one horrifying moment, she thought she spotted a dark lump by the pool house door, but she felt a wave of relief as she recognized it as a towel.

Slapping Casper's shoulder blade, Anna fell into a low crouch and sprinted across the grass.

Bullets whistled through the twilight, narrowly missing as they chipped ancient stone and shattered priceless vases around Alfred Harrington's opulent estate.

Anna dove behind a marble statue of some long-forgotten deity, twisting to return fire with methodical precision. Each shot deliberate, each movement calculated.

Casper flanked her, a few paces back, sheltered by a low garden wall separating a garden from the statuary; his own weapon—a compact submachine gun—spit out rounds in controlled bursts, raining chaos on the guards' positions. The estate garden had become a warzone, its terraced beauty marred by violence and the stench of gunpowder. Anna's left hand guided her rifle, fingers dancing over the trigger with ambidextrous ease. Her right eye squinted down the scope, scanning for threats amidst the madness.

The enemy was faceless, their motives obscured by the dusk and their assault rifles. They used the hedgerows for cover, creeping shadows weaving between the topiaries and classical sculptures.

Anna dispatched them one by one, her heart rate steady even as adrenaline coursed through her veins. She may have been discharged five years ago, but this—this was muscle memory.

A child's shout pierced the cacophony of gunfire, threading through the explosions and the cries of men.

Sammie.

The sound jolted Anna, injecting urgency into her bloodstream. Her head snapped toward the source, eyes searching, dissecting the mayhem until she found the small figure darting across an open expanse of lawn, dashing madly for the row of first floor windows in the house's outer wall.

"Cover me," Anna said, her voice gravel and command. Casper nodded, understanding implicit in the tight set of his jaw, and she rose from her cover, rifle shouldered, movements efficient as she sprinted towards the imperiled child, her strides eating up the distance.

The gunfire crescendoed around her, a deadly symphony she moved through with lethal grace. Something hot seared her cheek, her leg.

Shit.

She dove forward.

Her mind narrowed to a single focal point: the mission. Save Sammie. Neutralize the threat. Survive another day. There was no time for anything else.

Gunmen were everywhere, moving shadows with lethal intent. Anna took aim. The rifle kicked against her shoulder as she fired. One shadow fell. Then another. She didn't hesitate. Each pull of the trigger was purposeful. The sound of gunfire filled the air, but it was just noise to her—a background to the task at hand.

Move, take cover, shoot. Move, take cover—pause, let the smoke clear—shoot. Use the smoke.

One statue to another. One hedge to another.

Casper mirrored her movements now, following after her. His submachine released a spray of bullets that took down two men trying to flank Anna.

Three more fell as Anna fired three quick bursts with her rifle.

Casper moved with her, their movements synchronized without a word. He covered her flank, shots ringing out from his position. Enemy fire came close—a whistle past Anna's ear, a thud into the dirt beside her boots. She didn't flinch. She moved forward, step by measured step.

Sammie was crawling through a window around the side of the house.

Shit.

Two men were charging after the boy, trying to snag him.

"Cover left!" Casper's command was sharp, concise. Anna pivoted, sighting down the barrel. Two more threats eliminated. The recoil was a steady rhythm in her hands, each shot a chorus of precision and death.

They advanced together, a relentless tide. Their targets fell one by one. No words were needed; their actions spoke volumes. They were a unit, efficient and deadly.

Anna reloaded, her movements swift, automatic. The magazine clicked home. She scanned for more threats, her body a coiled spring, ready to unleash hell. They were getting closer to the house. Closer to Sammie.

The two men who'd gone after Sammie were attempting to follow through the window he'd squirmed in through, one giving the other a boost and leaving him stuck halfway over the sill.

Anna fired.

The man giving his comrade a leg up slammed into the wall, leaving a stain as he slumped to the grass, and the gunman in the window screamed as her second shot found his leg, sending him tumbling headfirst through the window into the mansion.

Sammie screamed.

"Pushing forward," Anna called out, voice even, betraying no sign of the adrenaline that hammered through her veins. Casper acknowledged with a nod, his own weapon sweeping the area.

Bullets pocked the ground, spraying gravel and dirt. Anna slid behind an overturned patio table, her left hand finding the grip of her rifle with practiced ease. Eyes narrowed, she peered through the scope, a small oasis of calm in a desert of chaos. Her breathing slowed; her finger tightened on the trigger. The reticle settled on a gunman's chest, barely visible through the foliage. A squeeze. A recoil. A body dropped.

Three heartbeats.

Anna transitioned to the next target. There was no hesitation, only the fluid motion of muscle memory honed in countless engagements. She adjusted for wind, distance, movement. Another shot shattered the air. Another threat nullified.

Casper was mere feet away, his back to hers. His own weapon barked its deadly reply to their assailants. They communicated without words—a glance, a gesture, enough to synchronize their intent. He pivoted, covering the angle she could not. His shots were punctuation to her calculated strikes.

A pause to reload. Magazines clicked into place. Two breaths to assess. They moved again. Anna rolled from cover, boots grinding on the stone path. Casper was shadowing her, his presence both reassurance and necessity.

A flicker in the periphery. Anna twisted, rifle rising. The world reduced to a narrow tunnel, her focus absolute. The gunman's face filled her vision, framed by the sights. She fired. He fell.

And they reached the mansion.

Bullets ricocheted off the weathered bricks of Alfred Harrington's estate as Anna and Casper approached the door to the house. The staccato of gunfire grew louder, more frenzied, as they neared the threshold where Sammie had vanished from sight. Dust clouded the air, mingling with the sharp scent of gunpowder.

Anna led, her boots pounding against the ground. Eyes narrowed, she scanned each window, each possible sniper's perch with a predator's precision. Her left hand gripped the rifle firmly, finger resting just outside the trigger guard—discipline etched into muscle memory.

There was no hesitation in her movements; every step bore the weight of her resolve. Sammie's safety was the single thread pulling her forward through this labyrinth of violence.

Anna reached the door first, firing a preparatory burst into the wood around the lock and handle before pressing her back against the cold stone wall beside it. She signaled Casper with a hand gesture—three fingers, then a fist—wait, breach, cover. He acknowledged with a nod, rifle raised in silent assent.

She swung around the doorframe, her heel sending the weakened door flying inward while her rifle led the way. Her eyes darted from shadow to shadow, identifying potential dangers with the ease of a seasoned hunter. There were no unnecessary movements, no wasted energy—every action was purposeful, every decision calculated for maximum efficiency.

The hallway lay before them, dimly lit and deceptively quiet. Anna stepped over a fallen vase, shattered porcelain crunching underfoot—a stark contrast to the thunderous reports echoing outside. This was enemy territory, every corner a potential ambush, every closed door an unknown variable.

They approached the first door, moving swiftly.

The door swung open on silent hinges. Anna's eyes adjusted to the dim interior, scanning for movement, for threats. Casper hovered at her shoulder, ready.

GUARDIAN'S NEMESIS

"Clear left," he whispered.

"Right's clear," she replied, voice barely above a breath.

They inched forward, weapons leading the way. A shout from outside pierced the air, followed by a rapid staccato of gunfire. Anna's head snapped towards the window, eyes narrowing.

"Upstairs," she hissed.

Casper nodded once, and they moved. Stairs creaked under their boots as they ascended. At the top, a burst of gunfire erupted from the end of the hall. Instinct took over. Anna pivoted, sighting down her rifle with her dominant left hand, the stock snug against her shoulder. She squeezed the trigger—once, twice, thrice. Three bodies slumped to the floor.

"Go!" she barked.

Casper bolted for the room where the shots had come from, Anna on his heels. Inside, three gunmen lay lifeless, but Sammie was nowhere to be seen.

"Anna!" Casper pointed to the balcony.

A figure darted across the window, along the balcony, a small shadow flitting after it—Sammie. Without a word, they charged.

Suddenly, a door swung open, slamming into Casper's chest and sending him reeling.

A man emerged, shouting and brandishing a combat knife.

Casper caught the wrist, disarmed the man. The two of them grappled on the ground as Anna leapt clear, her rifle coming to bear on the two entangled men, the barrel twisting like a poised serpent as she tried to find a clear shot.

"Go!" Casper was yelling. "Get the kid! I'm fine! Go!"

Anna didn't react. In that second, she found an angle on the assailant's leg and fired.

The knife-wielding guard groaned, jerking in pain as Casper spun him into a wrestling hold, both hands on the knife grip as he forced the attacker's elbow to its limits.

But Anna was moving once more, sprinting towards the balcony where she'd spotted Sammie. There was simply no time. She needed to catch up with the kid before he got himself killed, and the only way to do that was to run.

She emerged on the second story hall, glancing left, then right, dashing off in the direction she'd seen Sammie's shadow mere moments before.

An ornate door hung open a crack, and Anna kicked it open as she burst through, her rifle sweeping for signs of hostiles.

And she froze.

Sammie was standing, trembling. Chill evening air swept through open sky on the outdoor terrace Anna found herself on. In Sammie's shivering hand was a gun, and he was pointing it at a man standing in front of Alfred Harrington.

Landon Byers.

Anna's gaze took in the strange scene.

Sammie with his gun pointed at Landon. Landon with both his hands spread, a calming tone in his voice as he said, "Easy, kid. Put it down, let's talk."

Alfred screaming, "Kill him, Byers! Do your damn job!"

Anna approached, gun in hand. "Sammie!" she said sharply. "Sammie, calm down. Sammie, listen to me."

But Sammie looked back at her, anger in his eyes. He had tears there as well.

He was trying to point at the billionaire hiding behind the ex-SEAL.

Landon looked calm but poised. Harrington looked downright terrified.

"Sammie... Sammie, drop the gun!" Anna said. "Listen to me, buddy."

Sammie stared at her, wide-eyed. "He... hurt... my daddy." Sammie swallowed.

Anna stared. Those were the first words he'd spoken since she'd met him.

"He... said... he'd hurt mommy."

Sammie had tears in his eyes now, he was trembling violently where he held the gun.

"Liar! The brat is lying!" snapped Harrington.

"Shut up!" Anna snapped.

Byers just held out his hands in a calming gesture. "Look, buddy... just relax, okay?"

Landon moved suddenly, His hands darting for Sammie's pistol. The boy stumbled back, yelped. For one split second, he nearly dropped the gun, his hands clamping down on the grip rigidly.

Bang!

Landon stumbled.

The soldier blinked mutely, his hand fluttering to his chest.

"Ah… well…"

He stumbled, grimacing, then fell. The dull collision of his body with the ground seemed to drive all other sound from the room.

Sammie stared, horrified. A distant part of Anna was aware of the trauma of what had just happened—but she'd seen death before. Her mind would process what it meant later. For now, there was still the mission.

"Sammie! Sammie, drop it!" Anna called out, shuffling forward, her rifle still locked on Harrington as she stole glances to Sammie.

But if the boy heard her, he gave no sign of it. He raised the gun, pointing it once more at Alfred Harrington, the man who'd kidnapped him, who'd evidently killed his father, and who'd threatened Sammie so badly, he hadn't wanted to return to his mother.

"Boy… boy, listen. I have your mother," Alfred sneered. "Lower the gun, or your mommy dies."

Chapter 16

The terrace was a cold slab of stone under a sky bleeding the last dregs of twilight. Anna held her rifle steady, finger itching against the trigger.

"I have your mother..." Alfred repeated, the old man with his wrinkled features staring down at the ten-year-old boy holding the gun, edging his way along the terrace railing, his estate grounds far below and spreading out behind him into the setting sun.

Landon Byers lay on the floor, grimacing, drawing a brief calculating glance from Anna.

No blood. He was wearing his vest. Sammie's shot must have hit him just right, knocked the wind out of him. A professional like Byers wouldn't give himself away gasping like a landed trout, but now that he was recovering, she could see the pain on his face.

Anna still didn't know what to make of the ex-SEAL, but she had bigger fish to fry.

"Alfred Harrington," she said, voice low and devoid of warmth, "I know about the mayor."

Sammie's grip on his own weapon faltered, his knuckles white as bone. His breath came in ragged gasps that misted in the chill air. The gun shook with the rhythm of his tremors. She spoke in a calming voice, hoping it might relax the kid as well.

"What's that?" Alfred began, his voice a hollow echo against the backdrop of his opulent home. Each word he spoke was a stone dropped into the silence between them. "You're mistaken."

The sound of gunshots had faded now. A single glance over the terrace at the garden below displayed bodies scattered like bowling pins, and as she blinked at the grim tableau, Anna realized she'd caused this. The other side of her, the Guardian Angel and the Angel of Death.

Grimacing, she looked away.

Alfred's eyes darted from Anna to Sammie and back again—calculating, searching for an out. He stood there, tailored suit clinging to his frame, every inch the picture of a man who thought wealth was armor.

Sammie was sobbing now, hesitating.

Anna studied Alfred. He was lying, she decided. He didn't have Sammie's mother. But it was a guess... an educated one, dealing with men like this, but still a guess.

"Cut the crap, Alfred," Anna snapped, the weight of her words like a hammer to glass. "You used the mayor. You killed Sammie's father."

He glared at her. "Who the hell are you?"

"A concerned citizen," she shot back. Her tone softened. "Sammie... Sammie, bud, please. You need to put down that gun."

Her gaze never wavered, locked onto Alfred's dilated pupils. "You used the mayor to isolate the beryl mining," she said, speaking matter-of-factly, using truth like a floodlight, hoping to see what scampered out from beneath the rock.

She listened intently to the doorway behind her. Landon was still stunned from the blow to his chest or in shock. But the bulletproof vest had protected him.

Part of her mind, partitioned from the rest, still desperately wondered what the hell Landon was doing in Maine, looking for her.

But now, all that mattered was getting Sammie to drop the gun.

"Sammie, he's a bad man. But let me handle this. You should go, bud. Please... don't do this. You've got your whole life ahead of you."

Her words came out stilted, ringing awkwardly in her own ears. She didn't know how to talk to kids. What the hell was she supposed to do?

Beth would know what to do.

With a sharp, steadying breath, she buried the thought and took a step towards Sammie, almost touching his shoulder. But Sammie stepped away, still crying.

"He... killed... papa..."

Sammie's gun danced a jittery waltz in his grasp. His eyes were wide orbs, reflecting the fire of the setting sun through the window and the burning fear in his heart. The boy's chest heaved. Anxious sweat glistened on his brow.

"Easy," Anna murmured to Sammie. Her voice cut through the tension. Steady. A rock amidst storming seas. "I've got this. I know what happened. Relax, Sammie," Anna said again, softer now. She thought of Beth—how her sister might've handled this. Command and comfort twisted into one. "Just breathe."

"Stupid kid," Harrington was saying, raging. "Who the hell are you?" he screamed at Anna. "Do you know who I am? Do you?"

She shrugged. "You're the guy who bought stock in LDX Corp. You're the guy who killed the mayor for not going along with your plan anymore. What happened? He develop a conscience?"

Alfred just blinked, then sneered, his eyes flitting to Anna's rifle, still leveled at his chest, as he impotently chewed the air in his mouth. "Stupid asshole wanted a bigger cut. Hear that?" he shouted at Sammie. "Your dad was corrupt. Know what that word means?"

Anna's finger tensed on the trigger, a coiled spring ready to snap. Her voice was cold and level, talking to the millionaire like a slow child. "Alfred, he's scared. Scared people do stupid things."

Sammie's hand shook, the gun vibrating with his terror. Anna was fairly certain the boy hadn't even meant to shoot Landon and she felt far less confident in his ability to control his trigger finger.

"What about the hitman?" Anna said sharply, pulling both of their attentions back to her. "You triggered his device too. LDX makes those, don't they? Is that why you bought the company?"

Alfred was shaking, trembling now. "The hitman? Pssh. Idiot tried to cut me out, make his own deal with the brat's mom. I couldn't allow that. I just wanted my money back."

"What money?"

"The money his daddy stole. His mommy is holding onto it! Which is why we took her too. Until someone gives me what I'm owed, I'm going to keep coming. You hear me?" he screamed at Anna.

She shook her head. "You don't have his mother."

Alfred blinked. "Yes, I do."

"Not possible. I have her," Anna said. "Back in a cabin. Safe and sound. Left her ten minutes ago."

Alfred hesitated, mouth opening and closing automatically.

"Bullshit..." he sputtered at last.

"Yeah," she smirked. "But you hesitated too long, now, didn't you, Alfie?"

Terrace tiles chilled underfoot. And like a switch being thrown, the sun disappeared behind the horizon, chill night air coming to bite at Anna's cheeks. She held the gun steady, unflappable. Alfred Harrington stood opposite her, his back to the balustrade, Sammie to Anna's side.

Alfred's gaze faltered, a visible shudder coursing through him. His lips parted, but no words found their way out. The weight of his empire teetered on the edge of collapse, the absence of an answer speaking volumes.

Anna watched, her gun unwavering in her left hand, steady as the heartbeat of a predator. She sensed the shift, the crack in Alfred's armor widening with each ragged breath he drew.

"Sammie, just drop it," Anna murmured. "He's done. Your mother is safe. That's why you didn't want to go back to her? You thought it would put her in danger?"

Sammie sobbed, nodding once.

Anna felt her blood boil. What sort of threats had Alfred and his men told Sammie to make the kid this terrified?

The air thickened, every second stretching into eternity as Alfred wrestled with the truth clawing at his throat. A bead of sweat traced the path along his temple, the only sign of his internal turmoil.

Slowly, Sammie began to lower his gun.

Then it happened.

The crack of a heavy footfall sounded behind Anna, and she swung to cover the door.

GUARDIAN'S NEMESIS

Muzzle flashes and the crack of automatic fire sounded beyond the door, then Casper's bearded face poked around the doorframe. Anna instinctively put up her gun, locking eyes with her teammate as he called out, "Wrap it up! I have them covered but they're regrouping in the front hall."

And with hat Casper disappeared, his focus recaptured by whatever chaos he was holding back outside the door to the terrace.

It all happened so quickly, but in that moment of distraction, Alfred's instincts seized control. He had lunged for Sammie, hands grappling with the boy's weapon. Metal clinked against metal, the sound ricocheting off the terrace tiles.

"Damn you!" Alfred roared as he wrenched the gun free from Sammie's grip, the barrel now pressed against the boy's temple. It happened too fast for Anna to get a clean shot and she hissed sharply under her breath as she brought the rifle to bear on Alfred again.

"Drop your weapon!" the old man screamed at her.

His finger curled around the trigger, knuckles white with tension. Eyes wild, he searched Anna's face for a sign of surrender.

She met Alfred's gaze, her eyes steady and unwavering. A silent challenge hung between them, a battle of wills. His hand on

Sammie's stolen weapon made one thing clear: if he fired, it would mean the end for him as well.

Alfred's trembling hands had betrayed him, but it was the fear in his eyes that Anna couldn't miss. Fear of losing everything he had worked so hard to build. Fear of losing not only his life but his dignity.

"You know you can't win this, Alfred."

Alfred's grip on the gun tightened, his face a mask of determination. "I've lost nothing yet," He snarled. "And I won't lose now. I have too much to lose. Who the hell are you?"

Again, she ignored the question.

"Anna!" Sammie's voice cracked through the tension, a reminder of the stakes at play.

Her eyes flicked to Sammie. Young. Scared. His life—his future—in her calloused hands. The boy who had looked death in the face and still stood trembling but alive.

"Alfred, there's another way," she said, voice steady as granite.

"Shut up!"

The air thickened. Each second stretched out, taut as a wire ready to snap.

"Alfred, listen—" Anna started again.

"Drop your gun now!" Alfred was a cornered animal snarling against fate.

She could disarm him. But if she was wrong—if her bullet didn't find its mark—Sammie would pay the price. Or worse, Alfred might flinch, might end it all by accident or twisted resolve.

"Anna, please," Sammie whispered, his plea almost lost in the gulf between life and death.

Her hand shifted minutely, maintaining aim but considering. Options dwindled like the last grains in an hourglass. She had to decide.

"Last chance!" Alfred screamed, his grip on the gun tightening.

Her jaw clenched. Eyes narrowed. Focus. The world receded until there was only the man before her, the decision she had to make, and the potential fallout of each possible action.

"Okay," she said softly. "Okay, Alfred." Her voice was calm, almost soothing.

But her fingers did not slacken. They stayed trained and ready, betraying her words.

"Anna..."

"Trust me," she whispered, not to Alfred, but to Sammie, her promise hanging in the balance.

Alfred sneered, "You won't risk it."

"Wouldn't I?" Her tone was flat, unreadable.

A breeze stirred, sending a shiver across the terrace. Leaves rustled. Somewhere distant, a siren wailed, its cry fading into the night.

"Time's up," Alfred hissed, his thumb twitching against the steel.

Anna's heart slammed against her ribs. Decision time. Act or retreat.

Slowly, she lowered her gun.

It wasn't what Anna Gabriel was used too, but it was what Beth would've done. In that moment, Anna realized just how much her sister's missing family haunted her. She hadn't saved them. And now Beth suffered.

Anna couldn't risk another child's life.

Besides... she had chosen to trust.

"You know," she murmured, slowly lowering her gun, "It's amazing who people vouch for nowadays."

Harrington stared at her, wide-eyed, strangely excited. Sammie was sobbing, murmuring, "sorry," under his breath.

Anna's gun clicked against the terrace.

She maintained eye contact with Alfred. "There's going to be a brief moment," she said softly. "When you raise your gun to shoot me. That's when you're going to die."

Alfred was frozen in place.

She straightened slowly, hands raised, empty. She'd chosen to trust.

Was she going to lose everything because of it?

Of course... she hadn't trusted Alfred.

But Casper's word.

His vouch.

She straightened fully.

"Stupid," Alfred hissed. He pointed the gun at her.

As he lifted the gun from Sammie's temple and aimed it at her, that's when Anna's trust paid off.

She'd been watching him out of the corner of her eye.

Landon Byers.

Straightened now, groaning, clutching his chest. But his gun was in hand, and he'd been scowling at his employer.

Casper had vouched for Landon. Had called him one of the good ones.

Besides, it was a desperate situation. What other choice did Anna have?

It all played out in slow motion.

Alfred raising his gun, to kill Anna. Landon forgotten, discarded like a broken doll off to the side of the terrace. Sammie was crying, his shoulders shaking.

But Landon had a clear shot from his angle where he sat.

Alfred screamed. His gun levelled.

"Don't look, Sammie!" Anna yelled.

Bang!

Alfred blinked once. Twice. The gun fell from his hand. A round, red hole had appeared in the middle of his forehead.

He stared, confusion etched across his features. He took a stumbling step forward then back, letting out a faint mewling sound. Then he toppled back, his hip twisting and buckling as the momentum carried him over the railing.

Landon remained seated, gun pointing at the air Alfred Harrington had just departed from.

"I said no kids," Landon muttered.

Sammie fell to the floor, sobbing.

For a long moment, no one moved. Anna stared at the crying child like he was a strange plant that had sprouted up from the mortar. She checked her rifle, slinging it over her shoulder, wincing as Sammie let out another loud, agonizing sob.

What would Beth do? Anna was surprised by the thought, her tactical mind slowing down for just a moment. She couldn't just stand here. This was too much.

Anna awkwardly approached the boy, trying to think like her sister.

"Sammie, can you hear me?" she asked, reaching out to touch his shoulder. Her voice was soft but firm. "You're safe now."

Landon watched them both, his gun aimed at the tile floor, and Sammie sniffled and nodded, looking up at Anna with grateful eyes.

"We should get out of here," Anna said, glancing at the man who had just killed their enemy.

"Where to?" Landon asked, still not looking up.

"I need to get Sammie somewhere safe," Anna replied. "Then I can deal with you."

Landon finally looked back at her, his eyes narrowed. "Casper told you I wanted a chat?'

"Sammie first," she said. "Then we can talk."

The boy clung to her arm as if she were an anchor. Her instincts itched at her mind like a splinter, warning her she couldn't quickly draw her knife or pistol if a seventy-pound kid was hanging on her wrist. It took thinking of Beth again to quiet that thought. She wasn't used to this feeling.

Anna had often told herself, while serving her government, that she was serving as a protector, keeping others safe. But up close... it hit different. The small boy's trembling, warm body. His fingers gouging into her arm as if he couldn't let go. His warm, wet tears seeping through the sleeve of her shirt.

He seemed so vulnerable, and her heart panged in her chest.

She gave him a little squeeze. "Let's go find your mom, okay?"

Sammie nodded slowly, and she began to lead him away, back off the terrace, and away from the dead man bleeding on the cobbles below.

Chapter 17

The RV was parked near a small playground. Through the window, Anna spotted where Beth sat on a park bench, pretending to read a book as she studied the figures on the swing sets.

Sammie was there with his mother.

Anna peered through the window again. They'd inconspicuously parked in the back of the lot under the shadow of a large elm. Sammie was laughing as his mother tried the monkey bars with him. The two of them seemed to be enjoying a moment of blissful ignorance. A miracle in its own way after everything they'd been through.

Anna glanced to where her sister sat on the bench. On their way out of town, Anna had wanted to stop by, to let Beth see the good she'd done.

And Anna would've been lying if she said it didn't touch her heart to see Sammie smiling again.

She closed her eyes and exhaled.

"Byers, you think she'll even talk to us?" That was Casper's voice, a rasp edged with amusement.

Landon Byers' chuckle rolled through the air, low and confident. "Anna Gabriel doesn't scare easy. She'll talk."

She turned slowly, facing the two men sitting at the table.

She had them both on home turf now, and Landon had gone the distance to earn her trust.

But that didn't mean she would agree to whatever he had in mind.

"Byers," she said, stepping away from the window towards the table, her gaze locking onto the two men. Casper stood broad-shouldered and wearing his sunglasses, a smirk playing on his lips. Landon looked more like a kindly middle school teacher, his hands folded, wearing his flannel and speaking with his faint Southern accent. He met her stare without flinching.

"Gabriel," Landon acknowledged, his expression neutral.

"Alright, so you wanted a meet. Here's us meeting. What do you want?"

Landon nodded, but hesitated, as if considering his next words.

Anna wasn't in a patient mood. They needed to get out of Clearwater by the afternoon. The FBI was already combing through the wreckage at Harrington's home.

They'd left all the evidence they could, pointing to Harrington's involvement with LDX Corp, including blown-up photos of the device found in the mayor's arm.

But it would take time for the feds to sort through the wreckage.

"Why are you here?" Anna demanded, her voice terse. The weight of her past hung between them, heavy and unspoken. Her eyes narrowed, reading the lines of tension in their stances, the subtle exchange of glances. "Maine's a long way from D.C., Byers."

Casper's grin was all teeth. "The lobster's worth the trip."

"Only thing I'm fishing for is talent," Landon shot back, his eyes never leaving Anna's.

The banter fell away and Landon's posture shifted, a subtle realignment of muscle and intent. This was the Byers she knew;

when frivolity drained away, it left behind the solid presence of a man who understood the gravity of the world they navigated.

"Anna," he began, his voice now stripped of any levity, "I've got a job. Not your run-of-the-mill assignment. We're talking about serious stakes here."

She crossed her arms, her fingers brushing against the fabric of her jacket where a concealed holster would rest comfortably against her ribcage. She didn't need the weapon to feel the weight of his words.

"Big job?" she prompted, her tone as flat as the side of a blade.

"High-paying client," Landon confirmed, nodding once with conviction. "The kind of payday that sets you up for life. But more importantly, it's delicate work. It requires someone with discretion. Someone with skills that can't be bought off the street."

"Skills," she echoed.

"Trustworthy people," Landon emphasized, locking eyes with her. "People like you, Anna. People who understand the cost of loyalty."

A chill skittered down Anna's spine, but her face remained impassive. Concrete facts. That's what she needed. Promises were as brittle as fall leaves.

Anna leaned forward, the metal rim of the RV's table cool against her palm. "Details, Landon. I need more than just vague promises."

Landon shifted his weight from one foot to the other, a creak of leather under his boots. He shared a look with Casper, who leaned against the wall of the RV, arms folded, a silent sentinel in faded denim.

"Alright," Landon said, his voice low. "The job is a retrieval. High stakes. Not something we can afford to mess up."

"Retrieval." The word hung between them, loaded and locked. "Client?" Her question cut through the still air, clear and demanding.

"Let's just say they wield power. The kind of power that makes or breaks regimes," Landon said, his jaw tight. He paused, as if measuring the risk of every word. "They've got reach. Influence. And they're paying top dollar for discretion and expertise."

Influence. Anna rolled the concept around her mind like a bullet in a chamber. Influence meant resources, connections, the ability to move unseen or to shine a spotlight so bright it blinded. She understood influence. It was a weapon she had wielded before, both for and against those with power.

"Top dollar," she repeated, keeping her voice even. Money was a motivator, sure, but it came with strings, with chains. She needed specifics. Names. Locations. Timelines. Those were the bullets you loaded into your magazine. Those were what kept you alive.

"Exactly how much are we talking?" Anna asked, her left hand now resting lightly on her hip.

"Can't give details until I know you're in."

"I'm not saying I'm in."

"Listen." Landon leaned forward, his hands open and unthreatening. "There's no hidden agenda here. Not against you." He locked eyes with her, steady and unwavering. "We go way back. You're the best there is. That's why I'm here. And then to run into you at the plant like that?" Landon clicked his tongue and tilted his head. "Call it luck. Call it Kismet. Either way, you are *the* person for this job, Guardian."

Anna held his gaze, reading the lines etched around his eyes, the set of his jaw. Trust was currency, and hers wasn't given lightly.

"I'm not interested, Landon. I've got my own job. It's sort of an ongoing problem."

"Casper's in," he said, raising an eyebrow as if that might sweeten the pot.

Anna shot a look at her friend.

He shrugged. "The pay is really good."

She sighed, massaging the bridge of her nose. "Can't. Beth," she said simply.

Her eyes moved through the window again, watching the swing set, the children, and her sister strolling the park. Anna wanted her to see Sammie was safe. Her heart ached for her sister, who had chosen a normal life, and herself, who had chosen a life of danger, uncertainty, and death.

Landon's eyes followed hers, taking in the scene in the park, the beauty of the autumn leaves, and the irony of the children's laughter, oblivious to the secrets and lies that shrouded their world.

He seemed to understand her unspoken words, the pain, the choice, the decisions that had led them both to this moment in time. He spoke softly, "There's... another reason you might want to help."

"And what's that?"

He looked at her. "Because of the target for retrieval."

She frowned, glancing at him.

"The Albino," said Landon quietly. "I hear you've had run-ins with him before."

Anna tensed. She shot a look at Casper. "What have you been blabbing on?"

"Not blabbing," Casper shot back. "You told me to put feelers out. He's one of those feelers."

"Not sure I like how that sounds," Landon muttered.

"Yeah, well," Anna shot back, "Not sure I like the feeling of the two of you colluding behind my back."

"You want to find the Albino, don't you?" insisted Byers.

She hesitated. "And you know where he is?"

Byers' eyes narrowed, and he met her gaze head-on. "We have a lead. And I need your help to follow up on it."

The faintest hint of curiosity flickered in her eyes, but she quickly masked it. If this really was a way to get the Albino, maybe even settle the question of Beth's family once and for all... Suspicion flared and Anna found her jaw grinding in thought.

With a blast from his nostrils, Casper rose from his chair and stepped forward, concern etched across his face. "He's not bluffing. I've seen the intel. It's good."

Anna let out a slow, leaking sigh. She bit the inside of her lip, tense. A low breath escaped her lips as she considered her options.

Beth still needed her.

But if the Albino had shown up again... then maybe there was a chance he still had Beth's family. Anna didn't believe it, but what could it hurt to hope a bit longer?

Landon and Casper watched her, their eyes filled with anticipation. They knew Anna well, knew she couldn't resist the thrill of the chase and the satisfaction of a successful mission.

Finally, Anna spoke. "Alright, but no more secrets. I need to know everything. The whole plan, the risks, the timeline, everything." She studied Landon and Casper, her green eyes piercing through their facades.

Landon nodded, understanding the importance of setting boundaries. "Alright, Anna. We'll lay it all out for you. But remember, this could be more dangerous than anything you've ever done before."

Anna arched an eyebrow, a small smirk curling the corner of her mouth. "I've faced some pretty dangerous people, Landon. I can handle a little job like this." She paused, her eyes never leaving his. "But I need your word that there's nothing else going on. No hidden agendas."

Landon met her gaze, his own eyes serious. "You have my word, Anna. This is about retrieving the Albino, nothing more."

She hesitated, and noticed the way Casper didn't quite meet her gaze.

She frowned, but released a slow, pent-up sigh.

"I need fifty thousand, up front."

"What?"

"You heard me."

"Why?"

"I want to check your intel."

Landon blinked, sharing a look with Casper.

"You have some of your own?" Byers asked, his drawl growing a bit heavier with the query.

She pictured Waldo Strange the Third. He had claimed to have a lead on the Albino's location, and in her experience, information was king.

She needed to come to the table armed with some of her own.

And if that meant using Landon's money to pay Waldo his finder's fee, then she would have to bite the bullet.

She nodded firmly, simply. "That's my term. Fifty up front."

She extended her hand across the table. Byers stared at her open palm for a moment, then nodded, taking it with a heavy clap.

"Done."

The End.

Book 4 is waiting for you. Scan the QR code with your phone to find your copy of Guardian for Hire.

What's Next for Anna?

Guardian for Hire

Ex-Navy SEAL sniper Anna Gabriel is no stranger to danger. Having survived countless missions in the world's most volatile regions, she now faces her most perilous assignment yet.

Hired by a top-tier private security consultant, Anna is tasked with capturing an infamous arms dealer who has evaded authorities for decades. Known for his ruthless tactics and an iron grip on the black market, this shadowy figure has left a trail of dead bodies in his wake, deterring anyone brave enough to pursue him.

As Anna navigates a web of international intrigue, betrayal, and relentless danger, she must rely on her skills and instincts to outwit a mastermind who always seems one step ahead.

Also by Georgia Wagner

Once a rising star in the FBI, with the best case closure rate of any investigator, Ella Porter is now exiled to a small gold mining town bordering the wilderness of Alaska. The reason for her new assignment? She allowed a prolific serial killer to escape custody.

But what no one knows is that she did it on purpose.

The day she shows up in Nome, bags still unpacked, the wife of the richest gold miner in town goes missing. This is the second woman to vanish in as many days. And it's up to Ella to find out what happened.

Assigning Ella to Nome is no accident, either. Though she swore she'd never return, Ella grew up in the small, gold mining town, treated like royalty as a child due to her own family's wealth. But like all gold tycoons, the Porter family secrets are as dark as Ella's own.

Also by Georgia Wagner

The skeletons in her closet are twitching...

Genius chess master and FBI consultant Artemis Blythe swore she'd never return to the misty Cascade Mountains.

GUARDIAN'S NEMESIS

Her father—a notorious serial killer, responsible for the deaths of seven women—is now imprisoned, in no small part due to a clue she provided nearly fifteen years ago.

And now her father wants his vengeance.

A new serial killer is hunting the wealthy and the elite in the town of Pinelake. Artemis' father claims he knows the identity of the killer, but he'll only tell daughter dearest. Against her will, she finds herself forced back to her old stomping grounds.

Once known as a child chess prodigy, now the locals only think of her as 'The Ghostkiller's' daughter. In the face of a shamed family name and a brother involved with the Seattle mob, Artemis endeavours to use her tactical genius to solve the baffling case.

Hunting a murderer who strikes without a trace, if she fails, the next skeleton in her closet will be her own.

Also by Georgia Wagner

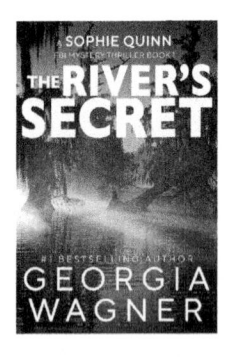

A cold knife, a brutal laugh.

Then the odds-defying escape.

Once a hypnotist with her own TV show, now, Sophie Quinn works as a full-time consultant for the FBI. Everything changed six years ago. She can still remember that horrible night. Slated to be the River Killer's tenth victim, she managed to slip her bindings and barely escape where so many others failed. Her sister wasn't so lucky.

And now the killer is back.

Two PHDs later, she's now a rising star at the FBI. Her photographic memory helps solve crimes, but also helps her to never forget. She saw the River Killer's tattoo. She knows what he sounds like. And now, ten years later, he's active again.

Sophie Quinn heads back home to the swamps of Louisiana, along the Mississippi River, intent on evening the score and finding the man who killed her sister. It's been six years since she's been home, though. Broken relationships and shattered dreams exist among the bayous, the rivers, the waterways and swamps of Louisiana; can Sophie find her way home again? Or will she be the River Killer's next victim to float downstream?

Want to know more?

Want to see what else the Greenfield authors have written? Go to the website.

https://greenfieldpress.co.uk/

Or sign up to our newsletter where you will get sneak peeks, exclusive giveaways, behind the scenes content, and more. Plus, you'll be notified of Fan Pricing events when they occur and get exclusive offers from other authors.

Copy the link into your web browser.

https://greenfieldpress.co.uk/newsletter/

Prefer social media? Join our thriving Facebook community.

Want to join the inner circle where you can keep up to date with everything? This is a free page on Facebook where you can hang out with likeminded individuals and enjoy discussing my books.

There is cake too (but only if you bring it).

https://www.facebook.com/GreenfieldPress

About the Author

Georgia Wagner worked as a ghost writer for many, many years before finally taking the plunge into self-publishing. Location and character are two big factors for Georgia, and getting those right allows the story to flow seamlessly onto the page. And flow it does, because Georgia is so prolific a new term is required to describe the rate at which nerve-tingling stories find their way into print.

When not found attached to a laptop, Georgia likes spending time in local arboretums, among the trees and ponds. An avid cultivator of orchids, begonias, and all things floral, Georgia also has a strong penchant for art, paintings, and sculptures.